TIDES OF LOVE

When her widowed father dies, Clarissa Marston is left penniless. George Farand, however, has a solution: in debt to the late Mr. Marston, he invites Clarissa to stay with his family at their Cornish estate of Trevarron until he can repay her the money. She warms to the genial John Farand, despite his darkly brooding brother Edwin. But Trevarron is a place of ominous secrets, and Clarissa begins to fear for her safety — until the handsome Richard Redmond comes to her aid . . .

PHYLLIS MALLETT

TIDES OF LOVE

Complete and Unabridged

LINFORD
Leicester

First published in Great Britain in 1985

First Linford Edition
published 2014

A catalogue record for this book is available
from the British Library.

ISBN 978-1-4448-2081-2

Published by
F. A. Thorpe (Publishing)
Anstey, Leicestershire

Set by Words & Graphics Ltd.
Anstey, Leicestershire
Printed and bound in Great Britain by
T. J. International Ltd., Padstow, Cornwall

This book is printed on acid-free paper

1

Clarissa felt as if she had been travelling since the beginning of time as she sat in the jolting coach that was taking her from London to Cornwall. The interior of the vehicle was gloomy despite the bright May morning of 1878, and its atmosphere — musty, reeking of old leather and two generations of passengers — seemed to suit the mood in which she had existed since her father died. She gazed from the window of the coach as it lurched and bounced along the pot-holed road that served as a highway. The countryside was in a wild blaze of beauty. Trees were heavy with blossom and flowers bloomed in the hedgerows; everywhere were signs that Nature was following its eternal pattern of evolution. But Clarissa was still numb with the shock of her father's death. Her troubled gaze barely recorded the wonders around her.

Tears filled her blue eyes as she realised that a phase of her life had ended. Twenty-five years had passed since her birth and, from the time she was old enough to think for herself, she had been blissfully unaware that life would change so drastically when both her parents were dead.

Her mother had died of a fever when Clarissa was eight — an event that turned her father into a brooding, taciturn man who shut himself away for long periods, leaving the upbringing of his only child to the servants in the big house in London. But now he was gone, and Clarissa was alone in the world . . .

After her father's funeral, she had returned to the house to find Miles Vernon, the family lawyer, waiting in the company of a giant of a man who was probably in his sixties but looked at least ten years younger. The stranger's blue-glass eyes seemed to pierce Clarissa to the very soul.

'Clarissa,' Vernon had said in a vinegary tone, peering at her over the top of his rimless glasses. 'I want you to meet George Farand, to whom your father loaned a considerable sum of money years ago to save Trevarron, Mr Farand's estate in Cornwall.'

The lawyer's bird-like brown eyes had gazed with ill-concealed distrust upon his companion, who approached Clarissa with a huge paw of a hand outstretched, while his expression conveyed a mixture of pleasure at meeting her and sadness because his old friend had died.

'Clarissa,' he said in a booming voice that over-filled the drawing room as his great hand engulfed hers and held it. 'I cannot express the extent of my sadness at the death of your father. Perhaps you are unaware that he and I were business partners at one time. The very fact that he loaned me the money which saved my estate and family from ruin proves just how close we were. Your lawyer' — he scowled at the watchful Vernon

— 'has told me how you are situated. Your father has left no money and you will, in all probability, have to sell this house for something smaller.'

'None of this sad tale has any bearing on the present situation,' Vernon had interrupted testily.

'Of course, my repayment of the loan will make you an extremely wealthy woman,' Farand had continued loftily. 'But unfortunately, I cannot raise the money at short notice, and it may not be possible to fully discharge my debt to you in the near future. However I do not come to ask for more time in which to repay. That is out of the question in view of your circumstances. So I would like to make a suggestion that may solve the problem to our mutual satisfaction.'

'I have already heard his proposal, Clarissa,' Vernon had interrupted, 'and my advice must be to reject it out of hand!'

'Please let me continue,' Farand had pleaded. 'My suggestion is that you close up this house and come to stay on

4

my estate in Cornwall. In truth, Trevarron morally belongs to you, for if you insist on immediate payment of the loan I shall have to turn the place over to you. But with a little more time at my disposal I am certain that I can clear the debt, and in the meantime, you'd be my guest and your presence would please my family greatly. In fact, you have been to Trevarron, although it was many years ago, and possibly you might not remember.'

'I'm afraid I don't remember, Mr Farand,' Clarissa had replied, looking into his appealing blue eyes. 'I do know that my mother was a Cornishwoman. Perhaps you knew her when she lived in Cornwall?'

'I did indeed.' Farand's booming voice had momentarily softened. 'At one time your mother and I were affianced.'

Clarissa was astounded, and naturally wanted to know more, but she fought against her curiosity. 'You must give me time to consider your kind offer,' she had replied. 'I am unable to think clearly at the moment. The shock of my father's death and the worry of discovering that I may be penniless have conspired to overburden my wits. But now the funeral is past I shall soon recover my mental balance and be able to think rationally about my circumstances and my future. With regard to the loan — my father must have thought a great deal of you to have made it in the first place — I am not disposed to do anything that would go against his wishes, so you can set your mind at rest, Mr Farand, about the fate of your estate. I will inform you of my future plans when I am in a position to make them.'

When George Farand departed, Vernon had made his disapproval obvious, and Clarissa's curiosity was aroused.

'You are very much against Mr Farand's kind offer, Miles,' she said musingly, 'but so far you have given no reason why you oppose it. What do you know about the Farands that makes them so unacceptable?'

Vernon had been reluctant to say, and tried to speak in general terms, but Clarissa would not let him off. She stiffened her tone and demanded an answer to her question. Vernon had shaken his head and suppressed a sigh.

'I have nothing but intuitive impression to guide my reasoning, Clarissa,' he had replied testily.

'If you feel so strongly that a trip to Cornwall would not be in my best interests then you must have a good reason for your opinion,' she had insisted. 'Pray do not keep your information to yourself, Miles. You are, after all, my solicitor, and if you have reason to suspect the motives of George Farand's invitation then I should be warned.'

Vernon had shaken his head. 'I have been your family's lawyer for more years than I care to remember, and my father before me. I warned your father against making the loan to Farand but there were personal issues at stake that need not be revealed here. Your parents are both dead now and their lives should be allowed to rest with them. Neither did anything to be ashamed of, so don't begin to think there are scandals in your family closet. As for my reason why I feel you should not go to Cornwall, it is simply this — George Farand is not a man of honour. He had failed to repay the loan he received from your father on advantageous terms, and any respectable man would have practically sold his soul to acquit his debts by now.'

Clarissa had considered Vernon's arguments, and, in the end, after some soul-searching, accepted Farand's offer. Now, after days of travelling, she was finally in Cornwall and fast approaching Trevarron.

She settled back in her seat and closed her eyes. She was certain she had made the right decision in accepting George Farand's offer. It would give her a short breathing space and help her readjust. It also afforded Farand the time he needed in which to recoup and finally pay off his debt.

The coach turned off the road, halted while the coachman descended to open a pair of black iron gates, and then went on through a cool green tunnel of overhanging chestnut trees that were festooned with tall candles of pink blossom.

Clarissa peered through the coach window, anxious for her first glimpse of the big house.

Presently they left the shade of the trees and followed a well-tended driveway that stretched across perfect emerald turf. Gravel grated under the coach wheels, and Clarissa caught her breath when she saw the massive house which stood four-square on the cliff top, outlined against a brilliant blue sky. The house was built like a fairy castle, with turrets, towers and buttresses, its countless glinting windows punctuating the Cornish flint walls. The front of the house was quite imposing; staunchly built to withstand aggressors. A flight of grey stone steps led up to a wide, heavy oak door.

Clarissa was strangely excited when the coach stopped with a jerk. The coachman descended from his high seat on the vehicle and opened the door of the coach, presenting an arm for Clarissa's support as she alighted.

The door at the top of the steps swung open, attracting Clarissa's gaze, and a tall, heavily built man with large features and dark hair appeared, followed by a second, younger man who was dressed in a dark livery. The younger man came down the steps quickly and, upon confronting Clarissa, bowed to her.

'Miss Marston,' he said, smiling a welcome. 'You are expected. Would you please go inside? Mr Farand and his family are awaiting you.'

'Thank you.' Clarissa ascended the steps, intuitively aware that she was under observation from at least one of the sun-glistening windows overlooking her.

'Good afternoon, Miss Marston,' the butler greeted, bowing slightly. 'I'm Osborne.'

He was a powerful man, probably in his late forties, and his brown eyes were dull even in the strong sunlight. 'I hope your stay here will be a pleasant one.' He turned purposefully to lead the way into the house, and Clarissa looked around with interest as she crossed the threshold to find herself in a great hall faced by a wide, curved staircase with dark, polished wooden banisters at either side. But her gaze was captured by the massive, tiered chandelier suspended high above the bottom stair; a straying beam of bright sunlight entering a small window on the first landing was creating a dazzling riot of scintillating light amongst the suspended shards of many-faceted crystal.

Osborne crossed the hall, his footsteps echoing upon the highly polished floor, and flung open double doors to reveal to Clarissa's gaze a large room walled by books on three sides; shelves upon shelves tightly packed with heavy tomes.

Clarissa noted her surroundings with a swift glance, for her attention was drawn to three men standing in front of the large empty fireplace. She recognised the huge figure of George Farand in the centre, and he came forward immediately with an outstretched hand, smiling blandly.

'I'm glad to see you here at last, Clarissa!' he greeted, taking her hand and enveloping it with his own.

Clarissa smiled as she looked up into his eyes, yet an unexpected pang of uneasiness stabbed through her at their contact; a product of her lawyer's warning.

'Come and meet my wife Lydia.' George turned, drawing her hand beneath his arm, and led her towards a high-backed chair which faced the tall windows.

Clarissa saw a tiny woman not more than five feet in height sitting in the chair. Her face was heavily wrinkled, wide eyes dark and probing, and despite the warmth of the afternoon, she had a heavy rug tucked around her legs.

'So you are Clarissa Marston,' Lydia said in a piping tone. 'I doubt if you will remember me, my dear, but I nursed you when you were very young.' She sighed and shook her head, allowing her gaze to slide away from Clarissa's face. Her left hand was tapping absently on the arm of the chair; the glinting rings on her fingers made sharp little sounds that echoed throughout the lofty room.

'I am pleased to meet you, Mrs Farand,' Clarissa said, and was shocked as she caught what she interpreted to be a gleam of malice in the old woman's shoe-button eyes.

'Lydia has been ill for some considerable time,' George said resonantly. 'But she is much better now, and with your arrival I'm certain her recovery will be all the speedier for your visit.' He turned abruptly from his wife. 'You must meet my two sons. I spoke of our meeting in London, and they have been awaiting your arrival with interest.'

Clarissa turned her attention to the two men standing immobile on the hearth as George led her towards them. Both were tall, and, quite surprisingly for brothers, completely dissimilar in colouring and build.

'This is John,' George introduced, and Clarissa found herself under the steel-grey gaze of a well-built man in his late twenties. He was tall and fair-haired, his face tanned, grey eyes looking almost silver. He held out a hand which was large and steady.

'How do you do?' John's tone was smooth and pleasant. 'I've heard a lot about you, Clarissa, and my father did not exaggerate your beauty when he described you. I hope you enjoy your stay here.'

Clarissa shook hands with him, her impressions muddled by an atmosphere she could sense around her. She felt dwarfed by his size.

'John is my youngest son,' George

boomed. 'And this is Edwin, my eldest.'

Clarissa turned to the other man, who was regarding her intently with dark, unblinking eyes. He was taller than John, obviously older — in his middle thirties — and dark-skinned. He had a black moustache that concealed the line of his top lip, but nothing could hide the sullen expression on his fleshy face.

'I hope you will enjoy your stay here,' he said in a tone which suggested that he had spent time practising the greeting. 'Now please excuse me. I must return to work. I'm afraid I'm the one who has to run things around here.' He bowed and strode to the door.

There was an awkward silence until the door banged solidly behind Edwin, and then George uttered a booming chuckle, the sound echoing eerily in the tall room. He clasped Clarissa's hand once more.

'I should have warned you about Edwin! You must ignore him,' he advised cheerfully. 'He's actually quite

15

shy behind that blunt tongue of his. But he does work extremely hard. If we could all work as hard we might not be in our present financial predicament. However you should not come into contact much with him. But John has been instructed to see that you do not get too lonely or bored during your stay with us.'

Forcing lightness into her tone, although she had been chilled by his words, Clarissa replied, 'Since our meeting in London, Mr Farand, I have been most eager to see your estate.'

'And so you shall!' George smiled benignly. 'But no doubt you will want to rest after your long journey, and Emily will attend to you. Please remember, Clarissa, that while you are here you must consider this house as your home, and if you find my family too much to live with then you can occupy an unused wing.'

'I shouldn't dream of being so unsociable!' said Clarissa emphatically. 'You've made me feel most welcome.'

16

'You should not have come here, child!' Lydia Farand spoke fiercely, startling Clarissa, for she had temporarily forgotten the woman's presence.

'Mrs Farand is not at all well.' George spoke sharply. 'Please pay her no heed.' He glanced at John, his blue eyes glinting like ice. 'Ring for Emily, John. Clarissa must be in sore need of a rest after her long journey.'

John crossed the room and tugged a bell rope. Clarissa suppressed a shiver as she looked at Lydia, who was gazing coldly at her.

George noted Clarissa's changing expression and moved to his wife's side, a smile on his face, but Clarissa saw unease in his eyes and there was sudden tension in the close atmosphere.

'I fear you are alarming our guest, Lydia,' George said evenly. 'So please explain what you mean. Why should she not have come here?'

'Her mother was here years ago! Don't you remember, George?'

'I remember very well.' A strained

note became evident in George's voice, but before he could continue there was a knock at the door, which opened to admit a maid.

'You rang, sir?' she asked.

'Ah, Emily!' George smiled as he returned to Clarissa's side. 'Come and meet Miss Clarissa Marston. She will be staying with us for a time, and while she is here you are to be her personal maid.'

'Yes, sir!' Emily came forward, smiling. She was Clarissa's age, small and inclined to plumpness. Her eyes were dark, her hair tucked under a lace cap. She was wearing a dark blue dress and a white apron.

'I'm very pleased to meet you, Miss Clarissa!' She curtseyed neatly. 'I hope your stay will be a happy one.'

'Thank you, Emily,' Clarissa responded.

'Show Miss Clarissa to her room, Emily,' George instructed, and glanced at Clarissa. 'We shall see you later, my dear, and I do hope you will find everything to your satisfaction.'

'Thank you for your kindness,' Clarissa replied as she turned to follow Emily from the room, and sensed the intensity of eyes watching her departure . . .

Emily led the way to the staircase and they ascended thickly carpeted steps. At the top there was a wide gallery, and they followed it for a short distance before turning off into a short corridor. Clarissa noted that no expense had been spared in decoration or furnishing.

'This is the guest suite, Miss Clarissa,' said Emily, pausing to open a door. 'I'm sure you'll find it very comfortable.'

'Have you been here very long?'

'About ten years.' Emily stepped aside for Clarissa to enter a spacious sitting room which had windows overlooking the cliff top and the sea beyond. The walls were wood-panelled; the curtains of soft green velvet, richly upholstered chairs, an exquisite sofa and a thick carpet underfoot completed the furnishings.

'Do you like being here?' Clarissa

19

queried. She felt the need to make friends with the maid, for her first impressions of the Farand family were a trifle confused.

'I like Trevarron very much, Miss,' Emily replied, shrugging expressively.

Clarissa listened patiently to Emily's chatter as they unpacked the trunks and put her clothes in the wardrobes, but she was feeling strangely troubled, experiencing a growing conviction that she ought to have followed her lawyer's advice and turned down George Farand's invitation to Trevarron.

Perhaps she was uneasy because she could sense vague undercurrents here.

'I'll call you when dinner is served, miss,' Emily said when Clarissa's clothes had been put away, 'and if there's anything you need, the bell rope is by the door.'

'Thank you, Emily.' Clarissa moved to a window to look at the vista outside. Directly beneath her was a grey flagstone terrace, which lay as a barrier between the house and the extensive lawn stretching out between the terrace and the cliff top.

Toward the rear of the house she noted that the sea had made an encroachment, crumbling the cliff until there was barely fifty yards between house and precipice. The outline of the coast stretched away in undulating fashion, and here and there, sharp-toothed rocks protruded from the calm water like black stumps. Clarissa sighed and backed away from the window to turn and inspect her suite.

The sitting room had two doors opening off it. One led into a dressing room while the other gave access to her bedroom. She was surprised by the luxury that had been provided for her. The bed was gilded, adorned with silks and lace, and there were exotic tapestries on the walls, while thick rugs covered most of the floor space.

When it was time for dinner, Emily came for Clarissa, who felt somewhat nervous as she followed the maid to the staircase and descended. She was shown into the dining room, which, like the rest of the house, had been furnished by Hepplewhite and Chippendale. The room was wood-panelled, and the chandelier suspended over the dining table was another example of supreme craftsmanship.

Neither Lydia nor Edwin was present. Clarissa paused on the threshold. George rose from the head of the table and came to her side. He was smiling, but Clarissa could sense his uneasiness. John rose and bowed formally as George led her to a vacant place, and he made a show of seating and settling her at the table.

'Well, now!' George spoke in a hearty tone which sounded quite false to Clarissa. He leaned over her, talking smoothly, and she froze inside at his nearness. 'It's a long time since we had such a beauty to share our table. Clarissa, you bear an amazing likeness to your dear mother. What a tragedy that she died so young! How long has it been, my dear?'

'About seventeen years, I believe.' Clarissa's eyes darkened momentarily and she caught her breath as emotion tugged at her. 'I'm afraid I don't remember too much about her. My only real recollection is of her last illness.'

'Death and illness are facts over which we have no control,' George remarked as he returned to his seat. 'I hope you will excuse Lydia's absence.' He sat down opposite. 'She rarely joins us for dinner these days. And Edwin is generally so busy he usually misses this meal of the day. But there are two of us here and we shall do our utmost to entertain you, Clarissa.'

'Thank you,' she responded. 'I must say I'm longing to see the countryside hereabouts. My father told me so much about Cornwall, and I've always been attracted by the thought of travelling down here. But I cannot recall the last time I was out of London, and I'm simply longing to walk along the cliffs and explore. There is a delightful cove below the house that I noticed from my window.'

John leaned forward. 'At high tide the cove is completely under water, so if the tide comes in while you're down there then the only way out is by swimming around the headland, which is not easy, for the currents and tides are treacherous.'

'And I never learned to swim!' Clarissa replied, fighting down a sense of menace. She was disconcerted by her feelings, and attributed them to tiredness, but sensed that an atmosphere in the house was overshadowing her.

The atmosphere during the meal was light and cheerful, for both George and John were at great pains to set her at ease. Clarissa was asked many questions about life in London and, in her turn, fairly interrogated George. John proved to be quite pleasant, maintaining the conversation easily whenever it showed signs of flagging.

By the time the meal ended, she found that her impressions of veiled hostility were fading, and tried to reassess the Farands. Now she was beginning to look forward to her stay in Cornwall, she was feeling unusually animated. The chilled dry wine which had been served with the roast had added attractive spots of colour to her smooth cheeks, and she felt almost light-hearted as she relaxed.

It was only later, when she was in her suite and preparing to retire, that she re-experienced pangs of doubt. Slipping between the cool, lavender-scented sheets, she found her thoughts returning to her first dismaying impressions. She had felt so tired before, but now, lying in the dark, sleep was dispelled by the strangeness of her surroundings and the unease in her mind.

Finally, she threw back the bed covers and arose to cross to the window, where she drew aside the heavy curtains, allowing pale moonlight to filter into the room. She stood at the window for what seemed to be an eternity, gazing down at the enchanted garden spread before her, watching the moon sailing across a cloudless sky in which innumerable stars twinkled. It was a perfect night; she stood enraptured until tiredness seeped into her mind. Then she went back to bed and slept soundly . . .

She awoke suddenly and started up nervously in velvet darkness. The moon had set and there was just a pale oblong in the night to mark the position of the window. For some time she lay trying to discover what had disturbed her. The silence was heavy. Then she heard a scraping sound, and stiffened when it was repeated. It seemed to be coming from the terrace, and she rose quickly and crossed to the window. The dark, silent countryside fascinated her as she gazed into the shadows, probing the fainter areas where the lawn stretched bare and level to the cliff top.

She tensed when she saw a dim light moving through the trees skirting the edge of the lawn, and for some moments she stared intently, watching its progress and wondering what it was until she realised that a black figure was carrying a hooded lantern. But who could be out at this unearthly hour? Was Edwin still working? Then fear stabbed through her, for a slight movement directly below in the dense shadows on the terrace caught her attention, and she stiffened as another figure materialised.

The approaching light was coming across the lawn, and by narrowing her eyes and peering hard, Clarissa could see an outline of the man who was carrying the lantern. He halted eventually, confronting the figure on the terrace, and Clarissa was exasperated when she could not identify either figure.

A blood-curdling shriek pierced the heavy silence, shocking Clarissa, and was repeated almost immediately. She froze in fear, cocking her head to pick up the direction from whence it came, and a frown touched her features when she realised that it had originated inside the house. As echoes fled, she saw that the lantern on the terrace was quickly extinguished and the two figures hurriedly separated. One crossed the terrace and entered the house while the other ran soundlessly back the way it had come.

Clarissa's flesh crawled as she listened to the fading screams. Lighting her bed-side lamp with trembling fingers, she carried it into the corridor, surprised that she was brave enough to investi-gate. Relief filled her when she saw John, holding a lighted candle, standing in a doorway just along the corridor.

'What on earth is happening?' she demanded. 'It sounded as if someone was being murdered!'

'It's nothing to worry about.' John's voice was tense, his tone belying the words he uttered. His face, shadowed by the light shining between them, seemed confused, as if he had been disturbed from a deep sleep.

'But the screams I heard!'

'It was Mother. She suffers the most dreadful nightmares, and normally I ignore the disturbances, but I realised that you had not been warned to expect them so I felt I should come out of my room to reassure you. When you heard those screams you must have thought there was a maniac loose in the house.'

Clarissa felt constrained to mention the figures she had seen, but the expression on John's face did not encourage conversation and she sighed and turned away, keeping her thoughts to herself.

'In that case I shall return to my room,' she said shortly, suppressing a sigh. 'Goodnight.'

John laughed. 'It should be good morning,' he responded. 'It is half past four now, and dawn is not far off.'

Clarissa shivered as she returned to her bed. She was deeply troubled, and slept only fitfully until morning despite her resolution to ignore the fears of her imagination . . .

2

At breakfast that morning George apologised profusely to Clarissa for the disturbance Lydia had caused in the night, and he was unable to conceal the disquiet that showed in his pale eyes, although his manner was bluff as usual. He had to make an effort to appear normal, and it was obvious.

'Lydia suffered a nervous illness some months ago which was, no doubt, brought on by our financial problems,' George explained, his eyes narrowed in their pouches of wrinkled flesh. He looked as if he had not slept much during the night, and Clarissa wondered if he had been one of those mysterious figures on the terrace.

'I'm sorry to hear that,' she said, surfacing from her thoughts. 'That kind of illness is the most difficult from which to recover.'

'My family has had its share of troubles, both personal and financial.' George spoke broodingly, although he smiled as Clarissa met his gaze. 'Please forgive me!' he apologised. 'I do beg your pardon. I have no wish to depress you with our problems. You are sorely in need of a change to your London life, and we must see to it that you enjoy your stay here. I promise you there is much to see and do in this part of the country, and John will attend to your needs, for Edwin runs the estate and I take care of other business. We have a tin mine close by.' He shrugged. 'It isn't showing much of a profit these days but we can only live in hope. Now, if you will excuse me, I must go about my business. John, you have my explicit instructions. See that you spare no effort to entertain our charming guest.'

John smiled, but Clarissa noticed that his face sobered quickly after his father had departed, and she wondered what was passing through his mind. She studied him discreetly. He was very good-looking. His grey eyes were very light, his fair hair curly and rather crinkled at the temples. He obviously did no work around the estate because he was well dressed. His hands looked soft and unaccustomed to work of any kind.

'I hope you don't find my father too overpowering,' he said quietly. 'He's trying very hard to make a good impression on you, Clarissa, but he faces many obstacles. It's tragic that we are so heavily in debt; I really don't know what would have happened if you had demanded immediate repayment. Father is an honourable man, and would have had no hesitation in selling the estate if you had insisted on an immediate repayment of the loan.'

'I hope my presence will not be a constant reminder of that particular problem,' Clarissa said softly. 'Perhaps I ought to return to London, buy a smaller house, and live quietly until your father's finances are in a healthier state.'

'Please don't do that! Having you here as a guest is helping father's peace of mind. He feels that he is doing something constructive to improve the situation, and Heaven knows he needs a hope to hang on to. The indications are that the Farand family is coming apart at the seams now. Father's brother Warner lives next to us on a farm, and he is always agitating about something or other. Edwin is restless and obviously dissatisfied, and he grows more morose with each passing day. Mother's health is deteriorating despite the ministrations of her doctor. All in all, we seem to be on a steady decline.'

'I'm sorry to hear such a tale of woe,' Clarissa told him. 'Perhaps it will all change now your father has had good news from me. He does not have to worry about repaying the loan immediately. I am looking forward to staying here several weeks. Cornwall is beautiful, and I'd be foolish not to take advantage of my visit.'

'So what would you like to do today?' He smiled, the harsh lines of his face momentarily softening.

'I'd like to walk along the cliffs,' she said without hesitation. 'The scenery is entrancing. I don't think I could ever tire of it!'

John nodded, and with breakfast at an end they arose and departed to prepare for an outing. Clarissa donned a light green dress and a matching bonnet. After some deliberation she decided to carry a parasol, for the sun was blazing down from a cloudless blue sky and there was very little breeze. John was waiting when she went down to the hall, and he nodded his approval of her appearance.

'You make an enchanting picture,' he observed. 'I shall be very proud to squire you when we make a round of the local social set. But I fear I should soon lose your company. There are a great many young men around here who will have their lives disturbed by your presence.'

She made no reply, but felt flattered by his words.

They left the house and crossed the terrace, following a footpath that skirted the closely cropped lawn. Clarissa paused, her hand upon John's arm, and her blue eyes sparkled as she gazed around. The air was heavy with scent from nearby flower beds. Roses were climbing a tall fence, their petals red and pink. A pale blue butterfly almost touched her face as it passed on gossamer wings, following an erratic course through the sunlit air.

'I hope you feel as happy as you look,' John remarked, and Clarissa smiled.

'Your father was right when he said my visit here would aid me as well as provide him with a respite,' she replied. 'I have never felt so elated.'

They walked along the cliff top and Clarissa was breathless with sheer delight. The sea was like a mill pond, clear and inviting, and the sharp black rocks showing just beneath the surface gave no indication of the terrors they held for seafarers when storms turned the rocky coast into stark hostility.

'There's a covered shaft a little farther along by which one can descend into the cove,' John said. 'At the moment the tide is on the turn, but it will be ebbing very soon, and then the beach will be uncovered. As you can see, down there at the moment we could not set a foot anywhere without getting wet. It looks quite picturesque, but that is Nature's deception, and it is a very dangerous place at the wrong time.'

As Clarissa listened, her imagination already at work and in her mind's eye, she could see the mighty Atlantic rollers crashing into the cliff under the thrusting power of a south-westerly storm. She drew a deep breath, shivering with anticipation, as John moved between her and the cliff edge, while they continued along a well-defined path. The air was as sweet as wine, the sunlight perfect for sight-seeing.

They passed a small shed on the cliff which John said housed the winching gear that lowered a large basket down the shaft into a cave which gave access to the cove. John did not stop for Clarissa to examine the shed, and they walked for perhaps a mile before leaving the Farand cove behind. When Clarissa was able to look into the next bay she saw, with growing delight, a little stone harbour in the distance which was backed by a small town. There was a narrow street that followed the gentle curve of the shore, with small houses and shops huddled along either side of it. Jetties protruded like black fingers from the quayside, each having fishing boats and other small craft moored to their seaweed-covered piles. Nets were spread out in the sun, and lobster pots were stacked high.

'That's Rynmouth,' John informed her. 'It's too far for us to visit on foot, but I'll take you there later. It's a beautiful place, and I'm sure you'll enjoy it.'

Clarissa saw him glance around in a matter-of-fact way, an action that proclaimed that he was not experiencing the delights as she did. He had probably looked at the scene too many times, she reflected, saddened because familiarity could blunt the senses. He met her gaze and smiled, and she was relieved because he seemed so friendly.

'Come along,' he said at length. 'I do not wish to tire you on your first day. We should make our way back to Farand's Cove and go down to the beach, where Osborne and Emily should be waiting for us.'

Clarissa took a last look at Rynmouth and promised herself the pleasure of exploring its narrow streets and the harbour later. They went back to the path leading down into the bay that was adjacent to Farand's Cove, and Clarissa saw that the tide had ebbed to leave yellow sand as far out as the end of the jutting arm that marked the southernmost boundary of the cove.

'The path can be treacherous in

places, so be careful,' John warned, leading the descent and turning several times to check her progress. However they gained the beach safely and walked to the water's edge, leaving footprints in the wet sand.

Clarissa looked around with quick, incisive glances, taking in the natural beauty of their surroundings. Seeing some dark holes in the face of the cliffs, she pointed to them.

'Smugglers' caves?' she demanded excitedly.

'What do you know about Cornish smugglers?'

'Only what I have read. Is it true that they don't regard smuggling as a crime but as a way of life?'

'They bring in brandy, silks and other treasures from France.' John smiled. 'There is local gossip about smuggling not being a crime, and it is a way of life for most of the smugglers. But the caves you see are not used for smuggling. These ones are flooded at high tide. I'll show you some further along the coast which have been used by smugglers as late as the last century.'

'Are you saying that smuggling has died out now?'

'It hasn't.' John's tone was suddenly serious, and Clarissa glanced sharply at him.

'Why say it like that?' she challenged. 'Do you know any smugglers personally?'

'I don't number them among my friends, and I'll tell you this much. I sense by your tone that you regard smugglers as romantic figures, but if we happened on any at this moment and learned their hiding places or their identity our lives should be in mortal danger.'

'So they are common criminals!' Clarissa shook her head as her romantic notions crumbled.

'That's one point of view.' He shook his head. 'And you look frightened now, which is the last thing I want, but life is not always as rosy as it appears. You have led a sheltered life in London! But some of these smugglers are men who cannot make a living any other way. There may not be work for them in the villages. Perhaps they lost their boats, or the fishing seasons have not paid them for their time let alone provided for the next winter. They have become desperate men with families to support.'

She nodded, chastened by his stark words. 'I understand. I was merely taking the popular view of smuggling. It has always appeared to have romantic connotations.'

'If you waited on the cliff top for a handsome young smuggler to row into the cove, towing a line of brandy barrels, you'd be a very old lady before you decided that your wait was in vain,' he retorted with a grim smile. 'Come along. We have to walk out and go round that headland to get into Farand Cove. The tide will be on the turn soon and the cove will be cut off until low water again. We shall gain the cliff top by using the shaft.'

They walked seawards. There were rock pools left behind by the retreating tide, and Clarissa wanted to stop and examine them. Some contained fish stranded by the tide, but John urged her to keep moving, and eventually they walked around the headland and went back towards the cliffs in Farand's Cove.

'But look, there are Osborne and Emily, waiting with the picnic basket I ordered before we set out,' John said.

'Has so much time passed?' Clarissa exclaimed. She saw two figures waiting at the foot of the cliff some distance ahead. 'They came down by way of the shaft, John?'

'That's right. I showed you the shed on the cliff top that covers the shaft that connects with that cave where Osborne and Emily are waiting. We shall have to ascend later by that method.'

'It sounds exciting,' Clarissa observed.

They presently joined the servants, and Clarissa was surprised to see rugs placed on the firm sand and a picnic already laid out for them. Obviously the Farand family believed in their creature comforts, she thought, as they relaxed in the bright sunlight. Emily and Osborne departed into the nearby cave to return to the house by way of the basket in the shaft.

John chatted pleasantly during the meal, and Clarissa hoped to learn more about his family, but he had little to say on the subject and finally sighed and arose.

'If you are not too tired, we could walk back around that headland to the right,' he suggested.

'What about the tide?'

'Six hours out, six hours back. We've got time to walk round the headland.'

Clarissa was doubtful as she glanced around. Time had passed so swiftly, and she was feeling quite tired. She was not sure she could face walking further and, looking into John's face, noticed that he was gazing intently at her.

'Perhaps you've done enough for one day,' he suggested. 'We'll go back to the house. We can be there in a few minutes by using the basket in the shaft.

Osborne will be waiting at the top in case we need anything.'

'That's a relief. I've thoroughly enjoyed myself even though I'm unaccustomed to walking this far. You'll have to break me in very gently to your way of life, John.'

'Please accept my apology for being so thoughtless.' He took her arm as they entered the cave.

Clarissa looked around with interest. There were storm lanterns set at vantage points in the cave, emitting dim yellow light, and towards the rear a great well-like shaft rose up through the solid rock over their heads. They stood in the bottom of the shaft and looked up. Clarissa saw faint daylight at the top, and by its aid she judged that the shaft must be at least one hundred feet above their heads.

'This is not a natural shaft.' John's voice echoed eerily. 'I rather fancy that some of my ancestors were a part of that grim band of men we were discussing earlier, and they cut the shaft

44

to link the house with this cave. I don't doubt that our estate was originally built on the proceeds derived from smuggling.'

He peered up the shaft, and then cupped his hands around his mouth, calling for Osborne, his voice evoking ringing echoes from the heavy silence. Clarissa looked up and saw a man's head and shoulders darken the circle of light at the top of the shaft.

'Send down the basket, Osborne,' John shouted.

Clarissa rested her weight first on one leg and then the other. She was becoming increasingly tired, and although she had never enjoyed herself more, she longed for the chance to relax in her room. Her neck began to ache from peering up the shaft, and she turned away, looking back towards the mouth of the cave where bright sunlight was playing upon the sand. Then she heard John gasp, and, as she turned to face him, he seized her around the waist and lifted her bodily.

Clarissa was too shocked to scream as John hurled himself away from the bottom of the shaft, taking her full weight as he did so. He stumbled, and they both went sprawling on the slippery floor of the cave. There was the most appalling crash. Echoes rolled through the cave for what seemed an eternity before silence returned, and for long moments afterwards they lay motionless . . .

When John finally arose and spoke, his voice was unsteady. 'I'm sorry,' he said, grasping Clarissa's hands and pulling her upright. 'There wasn't time to shout a warning. Are you hurt?'

She spoke faintly, her heart pounding madly.

'I've got some bruises, I shouldn't wonder. Whatever happened?'

'The basket!' John's voice was stronger now, but Clarissa detected a tremor in it. 'It descended much faster than normal and crashed right on the spot where we had been standing!'

Clarissa looked at the bottom of the

shaft and saw a twisted heap — all that was left of the basket. She suppressed a shudder, trying not to imagine what would have happened if John had not carried her clear.

'The winching gear must have failed. We would have been killed, or at least seriously injured, if I hadn't noticed what was happening.' He looked upwards and Clarissa did likewise. 'Osborne!' he called. 'Are you there?'

He waited for the echoes to fade. Silence came slowly and there was no movement at the top of the shaft, but the circle of light that illuminated the upper end was suddenly extinguished, causing John to gasp.

'Someone has just closed the shutter on the top of the shaft!' he exclaimed. 'What the devil is Osborne doing?' He raised his voice. 'Osborne! Answer me, man, won't you?' He called several times, but there was no reply from the top of the shaft, and when they looked up, impenetrable darkness baffled their eyes. John sighed heavily when he turned to Clarissa. 'If we can't ascend the shaft we'll have to walk around the headland after all,' he observed, 'and quickly, before the tide turns.'

Clarissa gazed at him, unable to see more than his bare outline. In her mind she could see again the level of the sea at high tide, the way the currents surged against the sheer cliff face.

'I don't understand this,' John mused, interrupting her racing thoughts. 'If it was Osborne up there he wouldn't have closed the shaft and left. And he must have seen the basket crash! He should have lowered a rope, or come down to see what happened.'

'Could the basket have been dropped deliberately?' Clarissa ventured, her mind reeling with speculation.

A silence followed, and she realised that John was badly shocked by her accusation. She remained silent, waiting for his reaction, and there was a long pause before he drew a deep breath and answered.

'I don't think the lifting equipment

could have given out just like that,' he responded. 'I don't really know what to think. Someone was up there when I first called, but now he has gone and we are stranded.'

Clarissa made no reply, and clenched her hands as John began to shout repeatedly for help. But the darkness at the top of the shaft only mocked the echoes of his voice, and Clarissa was so badly shocked she had to fight against pressing her hands over her ears. When John finally accepted that no one was above, she drew a shuddering breath.

'It's obvious that we will get out of here only by our resources,' she said stiffly, fighting to keep fear out of her voice. 'And if that means walking around the headland then how much time do we have?'

'We had better consider that without delay,' John answered harshly.

Clarissa did not admit that she was terrified, and permitted him to lead her from the cave. Outside, the sunlight made everything seem normal, and she looked into John's harsh face for reassurance, keenly aware of the shivers of fear that were tingling along the length of her spine.

John tightened his grip on her arm. 'If anything had happened to you — !' He did not complete the sentence, and she noticed that his eyes were filled with horror.

'If anything had happened to me, it would have been a lucky day for your family,' she said quietly.

He looked stricken. 'No! he said roughly. 'Whatever happened, it couldn't have been deliberate! You've had a terrible shock, Clarissa, as indeed, have I, and your imagination is now playing tricks! What happened to us was an accident!'

'And how do we get out of here?' she countered, peering at the line of the sea, which was a hundred yards out from the foot of the cliffs. 'You said the shortest way is to the right, around the headland. It looks a long, long way to me! Do we have time to walk that far before the tide cuts us off?'

'I don't think so.' He spoke hesitantly, apparently reluctant to face the truth.

'Then what are we to do?' she persisted. 'As I have already told you, I cannot swim, and you did remark earlier that if one is cut off in the cove the only way out is to *swim* around the headland.'

'That's true, unless someone on the cliff top sees us.' He scanned the top of the cliff, and Clarissa did the same, although the glare of the sun was almost too powerful for them to look with any certainty.

'This is a private cove, isn't it?' Her mind was frantically examining the possibilities.

'Yes,' he answered slowly. 'The cliff top is also private, so there won't be any people passing by.'

Clarissa was amazed that she no longer felt any fear; but she could not seem to accept the reality of the situation. 'Were not Emily and Osborne supposed to return here to collect the picnic basket?'

'Of course! But I'm sure it was Osborne at the top of the shaft before the shutter was closed!'

'Is it possible that when the basket crashed down, Osborne went for help?'

'That could be the answer, but surely he wouldn't have closed the shaft — !'

'So what happens now?' Clarissa persisted.

'You'd better stay here in the sunlight while I go to the bottom of the shaft and see what can be done.'

He re-entered the cave, leaving her on the isolated beach. She looked around desperately in the hope of finding a way to escape before the tide trapped them, and wasted many precious minutes looking up at the top of the cliffs in the hope of spotting someone who could be induced to convey a cry for help to the house.

Time passed relentlessly and Clarissa became concerned when John did not re-emerge from the cave. She glanced at the dark mouth of it in the steep side of the cliff, her mind filling with shocked speculation each time she considered what had happened.

Looking out at the sea, she was further shocked by the progress made by the flowing tide towards the cliff. A gasp escaped her. She was scared. She moved closer to the cave, calling John's name, but her voice echoed mockingly in the heavy silence and her concern grew when there was no reply. She glanced once more at the sea. Waves were breaking menacingly, and seemed to be much closer than the last time she looked.

'John!' Her voice became shrill as the true horror of the situation began to dawn. 'John, where are you? Why don't you answer?'

The silence continued. There was no movement and no reply.

When she realised that John was not going to reply she began to fear that a further mishap had befallen him, and tensed for what would be an ordeal. Re-entering the cave, her left hand extended for guidance, she hesitated, her nerves drawn intolerably taut.

She called frantically, her voice echoing, 'Please answer! Where are you, John?'

The silence mocked her. She clenched her hands, uttered a silent prayer, and forced herself to go on, eventually reaching the shaft, where the smashed basket lay in a tangled heap. Her eyes became accustomed to the gloom once more and she was terrified to find no sign of John. She fought panic and struggled to retain a strong grip on her faltering nerves.

Oppressed by the cave, she ran from its gloomy interior, wondering how it was that she was alone here. She fancied that she could see the bones of a grim plot. John had left her outside the cave while he re-entered to be hauled up the shaft by an accomplice, leaving her trapped for the relentless tide!

The sunlight seemed to mock her as she gazed around the deserted cove. The creeping line of waves was very much nearer. There was no sign of life anywhere, except for some seabirds calling and wheeling desolately. The cliff top, too, was deserted, but if John was in a plot to get rid of her then he might conceivably be up there now, waiting and watching for her last moments. And if their plan succeeded, there would be no one to press for repayment of the Farand debt!

She moved out from the foot of the cliff and peered up at its apparently unscalable height. The high-water mark was quite plain, about twenty feet above her head. But the foot of the cliff had been worn smooth and treacherous by the constant action of the sea, with no handholds anywhere to enable her to ascend out of danger.

She walked along the beach, and when she glanced at the sea she was horrified to see that the edge of the water was now dangerously close. She came upon another cave and her hopes were raised, but she soon discovered that it would also be flooded at high tide. She continued walking, looking for a path or a ledge that would offer her some chance of survival.

When she heard the sound of the waves breaking, she turned to check how close the water had come and her heart seemed to miss a beat. A succession of waves were speeding over the sand, small waves, but so numerous that they appeared to be breaking upon each other in their haste to reach dry sand.

A much larger wave came rushing up the ever-narrowing beach and splashed over Clarissa's feet, filling her with stark fear. She stared down at her boots, panic-stricken. A second wave rose even higher, soaking her dress to the knees, and she hastily scanned the cliffs again, praying for the sight of a human figure, hoping against hope that someone somewhere had decided to take a walk along this particular stretch of cliff.

Then she saw a narrow ledge, and what might serve as handholds in the face of the cliff which someone might have made while in search of bird nests.

She forced herself to take the first step, her heart beating madly, clutching at the slippery rocks and, inch by inch, she began to draw herself up from the sand. When she was several feet above the beach she paused to take stock, and was horrified to see that the waves were already swirling around the bottom of the cliff. Now there was no turning back, and she continued ascending until she reached the ledge, where she soon discovered that it was impossible to climb higher and she was still below the high-water mark.

She gazed at the smooth rock surrounding her. There were no handholds within reach. She lay on the ledge, her strength spent, and despair overtook her. She fought against panic and tried to master her failing nerves. There were shadows now along the cliff and she realised that the afternoon was well advanced. Time had finally run out!

It was then that she heard the sound of a dog barking on the cliff overhead. At first she thought her imagination was playing tricks but the sound came again, and she gazed upwards, calling loudly.

'Is anyone there? Help me please. Help!'

There was no answer, and she waited in turmoil of hope and fear. But there was only the emptiness of the coast, and she did not hear the dog again. Silence enveloped her. A wave dashed against the cliff and spray flew up, drenching her.

Her despair was almost complete when a voice echoed from above, and Clarissa caught her breath as she looked up. She could see nothing, but called frenziedly, and a man's voice replied, the sound of which brought tears of relief to her eyes. She clung to the ledge as a larger wave broke beneath her and she was covered in icy spray.

'I can see you but I shall have to go for help,' the man shouted. 'Have courage!'

Clarissa could not reply, and there was only frightening silence once more.

She clung shivering to the ledge as the tide flooded in inexorably, the waves rising higher and higher with ever-increasing ferocity, as if determined to sweep her off the precarious safety of the ledge and plunge her into the merciless embrace of the sea.

There were no handholds to help her maintain her balance and she leaned in against the rock wall and used her waning strength to wedge herself at an angle on the ledge. Risking a glance downwards, she saw that the ledge was covered up to her ankles. She had only a few moments before the sea claimed her . . .

A shower of stones crashed past her. One struck her shoulder, almost tumbling her off the ledge. She looked up and saw a man clinging to a rope being lowered towards her while the heads and shoulders of two other men were revealed on the top of the cliff, paying out the rope and guiding her rescuer. An eternity seemed to pass before the man came within an arm's length, and

Clarissa saw the rope was tied around his chest and pulled tight under his arm pits. There was a shorter length of rope, looped at one end, suspended at his waist, and he smiled reassuringly at her as he dropped level and quickly slipped a loop over her head.

'Both arms through the loop,' he ordered crisply, and Clarissa obeyed numbly. 'Hold tight,' he commanded. 'Use your hands to keep your face away from the cliff.'

Her rescuer shouted to his companions, and the next moment they were being hauled towards safety. Her senses began to fade as relief swamped her mind, but, before she fainted, one stark thought flared up in her mind. This wasn't the end of the nightmare! It was only the beginning, for if someone had plotted to kill her, then he, or they, would not be satisfied until she was dead . . .

3

Clarissa regained her senses to find her hands being chafed and discovered that she was lying on the cliff top under a shadowy sky. Her rescuer was holding her hands and, as her gaze focused on his face, he smiled reassuringly. He was strikingly attractive, no more than thirty, with strong features, and very dark brown eyes that were set under angled brows. His dark hair was thick and curly and his chin jutted ruggedly. There was relief in his expression as he helped Clarissa into a sitting position, and it was then she saw an older, white-haired man standing in the background, with such resemblance between the two that she thought they must be father and son.

'That's better,' her rescuer commented. 'Now we must get you over to the house. You are most fortunate! My uncle and I were disinclined to walk along this part of the cliff, and if my dog had not persisted in barking on the edge where you were stranded, we would not have discovered you.'

'This is no time for explanations, Richard,' interrupted the older man. 'The girl is badly shocked. We must get her to the house without more ado and administer some medical aid.'

Clarissa's teeth were chattering uncontrollably. She was badly shocked, and her reaction was having a sinister effect on her mind. She managed to get to her feet but staggered. Richard removed his coat and wrapped it around her, and then swung her up into his arms and walked hurriedly along a path that led into a large group of trees. Beyond the trees she could see part of a red roof, and was fearful until she realised that the house was not Trevarron.

'You've suffered a great ordeal,' the older man remarked. 'But don't worry. It's over now and you are quite safe.'

'I'm Richard Redmond and this is my uncle, Sir James Redmond,' said Richard.

'I'm Clarissa Marston,' she faltered. 'I'm a guest at Trevarron. I was down in the cove with John Farand.'

'I see!' An unmistakable stiffness edged Richard's voice. 'And what has happened to John?'

'I don't know!' Clarissa was overcome by a wave of emotion and began to weep.

'It's all right.' Richard's tone was soothing. 'No more questions. You are ghastly pale. What you need is a hot bath and something strong to drink.' He half turned, still walking towards the house, and called to one of the men. 'Ned, go to Trevarron and tell George Farand that Miss Marston is here, quite safe and sound. Hurry! Doubtless they're worried about her.'

They reached the house, and Clarissa was carried into the library and placed on a couch. Richard peered worriedly at her while Sir James crossed to a cabinet and poured out a drink before returning to Clarissa's side.

'Can you remember how long you were stranded in the cove?' Richard asked.

Clarissa began to explain about the picnic but Sir James sat down beside her and held out the glass.

'Drink this. You need something strong for the shock you have suffered.'

Clarissa thanked him and tentatively sipped the brandy while looking at both men over the rim of the glass. Richard was frowning and Sir James was looking extremely grave. She fought off a desire to weep, and drew a steadying breath as she tried to clear her muddled thoughts.

The strong liquid burned her throat, and some of the chill feeling that lay in her breast seemed to diminish and she felt slightly better.

'Please excuse my behaviour, for I am badly shocked,' she said hesitantly. 'You may think I am babbling, but I tell you that I am in fear of my life.'

The two men exchanged glances before Richard spoke. 'I expect you were terribly afraid on the ledge with the sea rushing in,' he said softly. 'But it is all over now. A hot bath and a good night's sleep should restore your spirits. But take some good advice and be very careful after this. Cornwall is wild country, and very dangerous to those not born to it.'

'Thank you for saving my life,' said Clarissa warmly. 'I cannot swim, and if you had arrived even a few minutes later I would doubtless have been washed away. But when I say I am in fear for my life I do not refer to the effects of the ordeal, however frightening, but how I came to be in it!'

'Drink the rest of that brandy and you'll feel a lot warmer inside, and then you can talk,' advised Sir James gently.

Clarissa drained the glass and Sir James took it from her. 'I have no desire to return to Trevarron,' she said unhappily.

Richard frowned as he studied her

pale features, his grave brown eyes unblinking, while Sir James nodded slowly, his face expressionless.

'We understand your situation,' Richard said kindly. 'Please don't let it trouble you. If you so wish, we will return you to your home.'

'I live in London.' Clarissa shrugged, reluctant to put her suspicions into words, but she had no inclination to return to Trevarron after what had happened.

'Evidently there is more to this than at first appeared,' Sir James decided. 'Please explain what is on your mind, Miss Marston, before anyone arrives from Trevarron. Meanwhile I do assure you that no one will harm you, and we will do everything within our power to help you.'

'It is not every day that I meet a damsel in distress.' Richard smiled, no doubt to reassure her, but Clarissa put her hands to her face and burst into tears. The two men exchanged glances again, and Richard shrugged helplessly.

'Oh, Lord!' he exclaimed. 'I do wish Julia had not chosen this week to take a holiday. We could certainly do with her presence now.'

'Let me handle this, Richard,' insisted Sir James.

Clarissa made an effort to compose herself. 'I do apologise, but you have sent a man to Trevarron to warn George Farand that I am here, and they'll be coming for me. I don't wish to see them, at least not until I have had an opportunity to consider what has happened.'

'That is quite easily arranged,' said Richard firmly. 'I'll have you shown up to the guest room, and when someone arrives from Trevarron we shall say that you are indisposed and cannot be disturbed.'

'Are you by any chance related to Henry Marston, who was in business in these parts years ago, and married Elizabeth Kingsley?' asked Sir James.

'Yes.' Clarissa nodded eagerly. 'He was my father. He died recently, and that's why I'm staying at Trevarron.'

'Aha!' Sir James nodded. 'I well remember Henry! I liked him. He was a man of great integrity and loyalty. When I warned him against some of his business contacts, he accepted my advice without question, and withdrew from those doubtful companies in which he had interests.'

Richard had moved to a bell rope, and presently a maid appeared, to whom he gave firm instructions.

'Please go with Lucy, Miss Marston,' Richard said at length. 'She will show you to the guest room and provide you with some of my sister's clothes. I'd say that you and Julia are of the same size.'

'And please try not to worry,' said Sir James. 'We shall take care of everything. I am the local justice of the peace, and you could not have fallen into more capable hands.'

'Thank you.' Clarissa smiled as Lucy conducted her from the room . . .

They ascended a staircase and entered a room where Clarissa was left to soak in a hot bath while Lucy fetched a change of clothes for her. By the time she had bathed and donned some of Julia Redmond's clothes, she was feeling more like her normal self. She had selected a beautiful cornflower blue dress with a lace collar.

'Oh, you look lovely in that dress, miss,' Lucy said admiringly. 'It's fortunate that you are the same size as Miss Julia.'

'Thank you, Lucy,' Clarissa responded.

Later, she stood at the bedroom window, watching the twilight closing in across the fields which were green with growing corn, her thoughts still on the grim experience she had suffered, and she could not shake off the chill sense of dread gripping her.

A movement on the drive leading to the house attracted her attention, and she caught her breath when she saw a carriage stopping at the terrace. George Farand alighted, paused and glanced around, and her heart pounded as he mounted the steps to the front door.

She sighed as he was admitted to the house, and stood as if frozen until a few moments later he reappeared, entered his coach and departed.

Moments later there was a knock at the door of her room. She went in answer and saw Richard standing there.

'How are you feeling now?' he asked, studying her pallid face and fear-filled eyes.

'I'm much better, thank you.' She noticed his gaze taking in her appearance, and colour tinged her cheeks. 'I saw George Farand arrive.'

'He wanted to see you, and was most insistent! But I put him off. Would you care to join us downstairs if you are not too ill-used by your experience? A bit of company now might lift your spirits.'

'You're most kind.' Clarissa was feeling better. 'I don't know what I should have done if you had been unable to let me stay here.'

He smiled. 'Perhaps I should admit to an ulterior motive. I have an unbounded curiosity, and I'm quite intrigued by what has occurred at Trevarron today. You see, when I asked George Farand why John had let you wander alone in the cave, he replied that John was in bed, his head injured by a rock fall in the cove, and was unable to answer any questions put to him.'

Clarissa shook her head. 'But I don't understand! John left me on the beach when he entered the cave, and when I went in after him he was nowhere to be seen!'

'Come and tell us all about it in more detail.' He took her arm as they descended the stairs, and Clarissa felt a tingle in her spine at their proximity.

They entered the library, where Sir James was already seated.

'I think it will be a relief to recount it.' Clarissa paused for a moment, her blue eyes darkening as she recalled her earlier terror. 'But first I must tell you that I suspect someone deliberately arranged the events to cause my death.'

Richard leaned forward to study her

pale features and, seeing no trace of hysteria in her expression, glanced at his uncle and nodded.

'Please continue,' he urged. 'Tell us in your own words the background to your becoming a guest at Trevarron and the subsequent events.'

Clarissa explained how her father had died, talked of the loan that had saved Trevarron for the Farand family, and described in detail her awful experience in the cove.

Sir James questioned her gently, reading from notes he had made during her narration, and his mind proved to be incisive, while his skilful interrogation brought to light further points that she had overlooked. Then dinner was served, and the questioning continued throughout the meal. Clarissa began to feel that her nightmare was over, aware that in the company of men like Richard and Sir James Redmond she could not possibly encounter more danger.

'I should like to consider this

business in greater depth and in solitude,' said Sir James as they left the dining room. 'I shall withdraw to my study to deliberate. It is not that I have to consider what has gone on, but rather how we shall approach the business with a view to gathering proof and discovering a solution.'

'If you feel up to it, I'd like to show you around my garden,' Richard suggested.

'Thank you, I should enjoy it,' Clarissa responded eagerly.

Richard rang for Lucy and asked for one of his sister's shawls to be brought for Clarissa. Then he led her from the house and they walked along the paths of the extensive garden. Dusk had gathered, the sun having passed from the sky and leaving a crimson legacy in the west that limned a few white clouds with magnificent golden fire. A blackbird was singing its last echoing song of the day and the evening was tranquil.

She looked into the shadows and knew a sense of security which had not been apparent at Trevarron. She trembled, unaware that Richard was watching her until he spoke.

'Are you feeling cold?' he inquired gently.

She smiled and shook her head. 'No — I . . . I was mulling over this ghastly business.'

'You must make an effort to put it out of your mind,' he urged. 'I am aware that it will not be an easy thing to do, but time should help.' He glanced around. 'Uncle James must have reached a conclusion by now, so let's go in and learn what he thinks ought to be done.'

They turned, and Richard held her arm as they retraced their steps. The sky had darkened imperceptibly and now yellow lamp light shone brightly from the windows of the house. The encompassing silence was intense, and Clarissa appreciated it.

'This serenity is perfect,' she whispered.

'It is something I've long taken for

granted.' Richard replied. 'But then, my sister and I live here very quietly, although I fancy that Julia will be marrying before the year is out, and I shall certainly miss her when she goes.'

'Your parents?' Clarissa ventured.

'They are both dead.'

'I am sorry,' Clarissa sympathised.

'This house and the adjoining farm belonged to our parents. Sir James lives at Belverdene, the family estate, which is close by.'

They entered the house. Lucy was waiting in the hall, and curtseyed. 'Sir James is waiting in the library, Master Richard,' she reported.

Clarissa could feel nervousness knotting in her breast as they entered the book-lined room. Richard ushered her to a seat in front of the fire burning in the large grate. Sir James arose from the desk, his face harshly set, and when they were both seated he waved a hand.

'Well,' he observed. 'This business will be easy to investigate, but we might do more harm than good by revealing our suspicions at this stage, so I need to know what stuff you are made of, Clarissa, and what frame of mind you are in. Could you go back to Trevarron tomorrow as if nothing had happened?'

'Uncle James!' Richard was horrified, and sprang to his feet.

'What would you have me do?' Clarissa's heart was thudding. 'At the moment I am still shocked by what has occurred, but if going back will help to bring out the truth of what happened today then I might find the courage to return.'

'You would be entering a hostile household.' Sir James's eyes glinted. 'But if you return, apparently none the worse for your mishap and without proclaiming your suspicions that some-one has tried to kill you, we might learn a great deal more than we could possibly reveal with an official inquiry.'

'Now look here, Uncle!' Richard interjected hotly.

'Richard, it is for Clarissa to decide,' Sir James insisted. 'I am well aware of the possible dangers, but we would be in a position to confer with her often. You could handle that, my boy! There's no reason why an unattached young man should not call upon a beautiful young lady whose life he has saved, is there?'

'If I called at Trevarron they would probably slam the door in my face,' Richard observed. 'The Farands have never been very friendly towards me.'

Richard looked at Clarissa, saw resolution in her face, and shook his head. 'Are you fully aware of what you might be letting yourself in for?' he asked.

Clarissa nodded. 'I am!' She drew a deep breath, for a decision had arisen in her mind without prompting. 'If you think there is no further danger for me then I shall do as you suggest,' she decided. 'I shall return to Trevarron tomorrow to see what I can learn.'

'You will have to be extremely careful,' Sir James warned. 'Eavesdrop when you can, and if you do learn anything at all then contact Richard as soon as possible.'

'It is easy to talk, Uncle,' Richard said worriedly. 'But what happens if an attempt is made upon Clarissa during the night? How could she escape their clutches?'

'Clarissa obviously is a woman of great resolution,' Sir James remarked. 'She can lock herself in her bedroom each night and no one will be able to get near her, while during the day they would have to be very careful how they approached her! She is now aware of their intentions so she can avoid all the obvious traps, like being alone in some remote spot. After the failure of this first attempt they will have to be more careful.'

'Whatever you decide, Clarissa,' Richard said. 'But I do feel a sense of responsibility for you, having rescued you from drowning, and I fear something terrible might befall you. To me, it appears to be very dangerous for you to return to Trevarron. Of course, I shall make a point of seeing you each day, but you will be alone and at their mercy for hours at a time, and especially at night.'

'I hope you will come and see me,' Clarissa responded. 'I shall always be indebted to you for saving my life.'

'Then it's settled!' Satisfaction sounded in Sir James's tone. 'Tomorrow you will return to Trevarron.'

Clarissa nodded, but clenched her hands as a pang of fear went through her. 'I won't pretend to like the idea,' she said. 'But I am determined to try and learn what has been happening, and now I ought to tell you about my first night at Trevarron.' She explained about the two mysterious figures she had seen on the terrace in the darkness, and mentioned the nightmares that Lydia Farand suffered.

'After this, do not be surprised if there are other mysterious figures lurking around Trevarron,' said Sir James grimly, 'but they will be police-men, Clarissa, so bear in mind that no matter what happens, help will not be far away.' He glanced at the clock on the wall, shook his head, and arose reluctantly. 'I'm sorry, but I must leave now, for there are certain matters I need to put into action before this day is out. I do hope it will not be too long before we settle this business, Clarissa, and I shall look forward to seeing you again very soon.'

'Thank you for everything,' she responded.

Sir James took his leave, and Richard, noting the degree of fatigue in Clarissa's face, escorted her to her room.

'I cannot pretend to like any of this, Clarissa,' he said. 'I shall be afraid for you every minute you are at Trevarron. I shall come to see you each morning, and if we make it appear that we have become close friends then it may serve to give you some protection.'

'How shall I ever be able to thank you?' A slight quiver sounded in her voice.

'It may be that Uncle and I will be

thanking you before this business is at an end,' he replied, taking her hand. 'But that's enough talking for one day. You look utterly spent, and a good night's sleep will restore your nerve. Goodnight, my dear Clarissa. Sleep well!'

'Goodnight, Richard,' she replied, and a sigh escaped her as she entered the bedroom. Tonight she would sleep peacefully, secure in the knowledge that she would awaken unharmed next morning with Richard nearby, but when she returned to Trevarron a new ordeal would begin, and she would be afraid to close her eyes in slumber under the Farand roof . . .

4

Next morning, when it was time to return to Trevarron, Clarissa's face was pale but resolute as Richard helped her into a coach, although she maintained a calm manner. He chatted easily, but Clarissa sensed that he, too, was on edge. His handsome face was grim, his eyes filled with a harsh gleam.

When they reached Trevarron, Clarissa felt an icy hand of anticipation begin squeezing inexorably around her heart.

'That's Doctor Walmer's carriage,' Richard observed when they alighted and saw another coach drawn up at the terrace steps. 'Has John taken a turn for the worse?'

'Perhaps Lydia has had another attack,' Clarissa suggested tremulously.

The front door swung open as they reached it and Osborne appeared. His face was unsmiling; his dark eyes bleak. He bowed formally.

She crossed the threshold with Richard at her side and saw Edwin standing at the foot of the stairs talking to Emily. He gazed in their direction, and came forward instantly, dark eyes narrowed under beetling brows.

'What happened yesterday?' he demanded, his tone almost bullying. 'How was it you were alone in the cove, and John was found trussed and beaten half to death in the shed over the cliff shaft?'

'Do you expect Clarissa to be aware of events that took place out of her sight?' Richard demanded, and Clarissa, watching the two men closely, fancied that there was bad blood of long standing between them.

'How is John this morning?' Clarissa asked.

'He's concussed!' Edwin glowered at her, and kept glancing towards the staircase. 'The doctor is with him now. I'm waiting to hear what he's got to say before going about my work.'

At that moment, two figures appeared at the top of the staircase, and Clarissa's heart lurched sickeningly when she saw that one of them was George Farand. She assumed the other was the doctor.

George's expression hardened when he saw Clarissa, and she was shocked by his appearance; his face was haggard, and he looked as if he had not slept at all during the dark hours.

'Clarissa! I'm so relieved to see you!' George glanced at Richard but did not acknowledge his presence as he grasped Clarissa's hand. 'This is a bad business!' he continued. 'We don't know what happened, and I'm hoping you can throw some light upon it. Osborne and Emily came up the shaft after bringing your picnic to you, and when you and John failed to arrive later, we began a search. John was discovered bound and unconscious in the shed covering the shaft.' He paused, shaking his head, and glanced at Richard. 'I understand that we have you to thank for saving Clarissa's life, and I thank the Lord that you were at hand to rescue her.'

Clarissa suppressed a shudder as George's words forced her to relive the awful moments when she had been trapped in the cove. She explained in a low tone the events that led to John's disappearance in the cave.

'A figure was at the top of the shaft after the basket crashed?' George asked.

'Oh yes! I saw him plainly.' Her voice shook and she fell silent. 'But I couldn't identify it, or even tell if it was a man or a woman.'

Relief glinted momentarily in George's features, and he nodded. Edwin grunted and turned to depart, slamming the front door as he left; a sound that echoed through the hall and set the crystal chandelier protesting musically.

'So John left you on the beach while he went back into the cave?' George watched Clarissa with a harsh gaze.

'Yes.' Clarissa suppressed a shiver at the recollection. 'I didn't relish going back into the cave. It was dank and gloomy and I had lost my nerve. But minutes later, when John did not reappear, I went in to look for him and he was not to be seen. I assumed that Osborne had returned, pulled John up on a rope, and left me.'

George frowned. 'Why should they have left you, knowing the tide was coming in? That would have meant your certain death!'

Clarissa shook her head, unable to think of a suitable answer, and Richard moved impatiently at her side.

'What does Osborne have to say about his part in this business?' Richard said.

George shook his head. 'He and Emily returned to the house immediately after leaving John and Clarissa on the beach, and neither left again until we started the search later.'

'Then *who* was at the top of the shaft?' Clarissa asked. 'And how did John get up the shaft after he left me outside the cave?'

'Those questions, unfortunately, we

are unable to answer at the moment,' George said. 'That's why I have sent for the police. I hope they will be able to discover what happened.'

'And how is John this morning?' Richard inquired.

'He has regained consciousness, but is unable to tell us anything because he is suffering from concussion,' Doctor Walmer reported. He was a tall distinguished-looking man with keen blue eyes and a weathered face. 'John's skull must be exceptionally thick. The blows he suffered would have fatally broken the head of another man. I shall report the incident to the police. It was a most serious attack.'

'I'll see you out, Doctor,' George said quietly, and he and the doctor walked to the door.

Clarissa looked at Richard, saw worry in his expression, and knew that she would need all her courage to go through with what had been planned. She longed to beg him to take her away immediately, but, despite her fears, she had no intention of going back on her word.

'I'll come and see you tomorrow, Clarissa,' Richard said as George returned.

'Yes.' She nodded emphatically. 'Please do!'

She accompanied him to the door, and he grasped her hand for a moment, squeezing her fingers reassuringly. Clarissa wished he could stay longer, for she dreaded being left alone at the mercy of this unusual family. But Richard departed and, reluctantly closing the door after him, she turned to find George waiting for her.

'Come and see John,' George invited, his voice echoing in the lofty space of the hall, and he continued in a slightly different tone as he ascended the stairs. 'I have no idea what you must be thinking about this business. In fact, I hardly know what to make of it myself. The basket crashing down the shaft can be explained as an accident, but what happened to John afterwards leads me to the only logical conclusion.'

'Which is?' Clarissa prompted.

'That one of our enemies is responsible! I'm afraid we have many enemies in this locality, Clarissa, and it was unfortunate that you were with John when the cowardly attack was made on him.'

She considered his words as he ascended the upper staircase, and concluded that the opposite was probably true. If someone had meant to harm John then he would not have been removed from the shaft. He would have been left as he was for the incoming tide to do its lethal work.

'I warn you that John is not a pretty sight,' George said, pausing at the door of the room. 'And you, Clarissa? I brought you here for a pleasant holiday, to help you forget the grief you suffered back in London. I feel responsible for you, a guest living in my home. Are you sure you wouldn't prefer to return to London?'

'I'd rather not leave at this stage,' she

said. 'I'm sure it was all just an accident, and I'd like to stay on if I may.'

Relief showed in George's heavy face, and Clarissa experienced a pang of fear as she saw it. Of course they would not want her to leave now! But she knew that as the first attempt to kill her had failed, they would have to be extremely careful over their subsequent actions.

Clarissa was shocked as she stood at the foot of John's bed and gazed at his pallid features. There were so many bruises and lacerations on his face! She realised that she had suspected John of being in league with the guilty person — that he had been hauled to safety out of the cave before being bound and superficially beaten for the sake of appearances. But the extent of his injuries made her aware that this could not possibly be so. He would not have endured such heavy blows for the sake of appearing innocent. Indeed, it was a miracle that he had not died from his injuries.

As they left the room, Clarissa looked at George's grim face. 'What kind of enemies do you have who could do such a thing?' she asked.

'Business enemies!' George shook his head. 'That is where our trouble stems from.'

Clarissa found it difficult to accept that other incidents might well occur, all with the same intention — to kill her! But she could not believe that none of the Farands intended her harm. Yet, would John's life have been put to such risk if others of his family had planned her death?

Her thoughts were deep and troubled, and she was startled when George patted her arm. He was smiling ruefully.

'I see that you are still badly shocked by your experience,' he observed. 'I suggest you go to your room and try to relax.'

'I intend to. But if the police are being called in then won't I be needed to tell them my story?'

'I'll endeavour to spare you as much as possible.'

'I want to do all I can to help catch the culprit,' she said with an air of confidence that she was far from feeling.

'You have spirit!' George acknowledged.

'Do you have any idea who might be responsible for what has happened?'

'I have my suspicions.' He shrugged. 'But you need have no worry for your safety in future. I shall see to it that you are not left alone or in any situation where some harm may befall you. It was fortunate that Richard Redmond was on the cliff at the right moment. Did you tell him you had been left in the cove?'

'I cannot recall what I said when he rescued me.'

George nodded as he turned away. 'It's a good thing that we Farands have hard heads. Now you must try to rest. If the police do need to talk to you I'll send Emily for you.'

Thanking him, Clarissa turned and went along to her room, sagging limply against the door after entering, as reaction caught up with her. She crossed to the bed and sank wearily upon it, trying to concentrate on what Sir James has told her to do. It had all seemed so simple when they talked it over but now Clarissa realised that she would find her given task difficult and perilous.

A knock at the door startled her and made her aware that her nerves had suffered from her grim experience. She went in answer to find Emily outside. The maid, looking ill at ease, could hardly meet Clarissa's gaze.

'Is there anything I can do for you, miss?' she asked.

'There is nothing I need but information, Emily,' Clarissa replied. 'Tell me what happened after you and Osborne left the cove.'

'Why, nothing, miss! We ascended the shaft and returned to the house. Mr

Osborne was to go back later for the picnic basket.'

'But he didn't do that,' Clarissa said sharply. 'It wasn't until Mr George began to fear for John and me that any of the servants left the house.'

'That's right, Miss. We had other duties.' A sullen note sounded in Emily's voice, and Clarissa detected it.

'Why was the basket left up the shaft after you and Osborne ascended? I would have thought it should have been left in the lowered position because we were in the cove.'

'Osborne said you and Mr John would walk around the cove before the tide came in. That was the reason for the picnic in the cove, so you'd have enough time afterwards to complete the walk.'

Clarissa realised that she would learn nothing new and frustration added its own tension to her state of mind. 'It was extremely fortunate for you and Osborne that the basket did not

94

collapse when you were using it,' she observed.

'There was nothing wrong with the basket or the lifting-gear at the time, miss!' Emily's dark gaze rested on Clarissa's face for a moment before sliding uneasily away. 'After Mr John was discovered, it was seen that the equipment had been tampered with, and it could only have been done after we ascended.'

Emily looked uncomfortable, and turned to the door as if to leave.

'Don't go,' Clarissa said sharply. 'Tell me, Emily, have there been other incidents involving members of this family before my arrival?'

'I — I can't tell you anything, miss,' she faltered. 'Mr George warned us to say nothing about what happens on the estate.'

'I admire your loyalty, but I think it misguided. I am not an outsider, Emily. I am a guest in this house — I'm sure Mr George has told you to do whatever you can for me.'

'There isn't much I can tell!' Doubt crept into Emily's voice. 'There has always been trouble around here for the Farands.' She shook her head. 'Strange things have happened and we had to accept them. Just look at Mrs Farand. They say her condition is the result of a foreign fever.'

'And wasn't it?' Clarissa prompted.

'There's a curse on the Farand family. That's a regular saying of Mrs Farand. You haven't met Warner Farand yet, have you?'

'No.' Clarissa shook her head. 'But I have heard of him.'

'Mr George's younger brother — he owns the adjacent farm, and he's a man who has to be watched at all times, they say.'

'Are you trying to tell me that he might be responsible for what happened to John and me?'

Emily shrugged. 'Everyone knew that Mistress Lydia loved Warner, and would have married him if Elizabeth Kingsley had married Mr George. But when your mother went off with your father, Lydia was pressured into marrying Mr George, and there's been bad blood between Warner and him ever since.' Emily sighed and fell silent.

Clarissa frowned, recalling George's words that he and her mother had once been engaged. Now she could begin to understand why her father had made the loan to George on such ridiculous terms!

'Can I go now, miss?' Emily pleaded. 'What I've said is common knowledge, but if Mr George learns that I've told you anything at all I'd lose my job, and that's a fact, and I can't afford to be out of work. My mother has three children under the age of six years and my father hasn't had a job since last summer. They badly need my wage, miss.'

'Very well, Emily. You may return to your duties.'

'Thank you kindly, miss.' Emily curtseyed and departed thankfully.

Clarissa walked to the bedroom window to peer at the spot where she had seen the two shadowy figures in the night. Emily had made it clear that she was afraid for her job, but Clarissa realised that if she let fear overwhelm her she would be afraid for her life!

5

Clarissa had never known such a long day as the one she experienced back at Trevarron. The hours passed so slowly, and although nothing untoward occurred she was unconvinced that she was safe. She ate lunch with George, which was an unduly nerve-racking affair. The afternoon stretched unbroken before her, and she realised that Richard was in the forefront of her thoughts as she remained within the confines of her room. She yearned for his company, and the awareness surprised her. But her thoughts were far-ranging, and she was startled later, when there was a knock at her door. Hurrying to unlock it, she saw a somewhat apprehensive Emily standing outside.

'If you please, miss, Sergeant Cake-bread of the constabulary is in the library, and he would like to ask you some questions. Do you feel well enough to see him?'

Clarissa was delighted, and followed Emily down to the library, where an insignificant little man with birdlike brown eyes and a bushy moustache confronted her.

'Miss Marston, I am pleased to make your acquaintance,' he greeted her in a voice that sounded like a broken reed. He smiled as he crossed the room to shake her hand. 'Please sit by the window. I hope you have quite recovered from you ordeal.'

'I am feeling much better now,' Clarissa replied.

'Good. I have talked to Sir James, and Mr Richard Redmond explained how he came upon you stranded on the cliff at Farand Cove, and I have been instructed by Sir James to investigate the circumstances of the incident that led up to your plight on that cliff. If you are sufficiently recovered perhaps you would explain the events of yesterday as they occurred.'

Clarissa steeled herself to relive the ordeal, and was relieved that she and the police sergeant were alone. Her voice was low but determined as she explained what had happened, and Sergeant Cakebread did not interrupt her narrative. His dark eyes were shrewd and, when she lapsed into silence, he questioned her like a dog worrying a bone until he was satisfied with what he had elicited. He studied his notes before his dark gaze lifted to regard Clarissa steadily.

'Are you certain that you have told me everything?' he asked. 'It is sometimes difficult to recall all the details at first, so perhaps you would let me know if anything else should come to mind later.'

'I'll certainly let you know if I do think of anything more,' she said. 'But what do you make of these events?'

'I couldn't possibly say at this stage. Only when I have all the facts shall I be able to make an assessment. Now, if you will excuse me, I must see if it is possible to talk to John Farand.' He smiled as he shook her hand. 'Try not to worry too much about what has happened.'

Clarissa was relieved when she returned to the sanctuary of her room, and remained there until dinner was announced. She went down to the dining room, but paused outside the door, which was ajar, because two male voices were talking loudly inside. In fact, Clarissa at first thought they were arguing. Then George Farand's booming voice commanded Edwin to be silent. Edwin, in his usual surly tone, snapped in reply.

'That girl should not have been brought here in the first place, and ought to be sent back to where she came from before this day is out!'

'I told you to be quiet!' George retorted. 'And leave this matter to my judgement. It will be settled one way or another.'

Silence ensued, and Clarissa pushed the door wider and entered to discover George and Edwin seated at the long table. George frowned at Edwin as if to warn against further conversation before rising to greet her. Edwin merely nodded a scant acknowledgement.

She seated herself and patiently endured the seemingly endless period during which the meal was served and then eaten. Afterwards she returned to her room, her mind feasting on the snippet of conversation that she had overheard between the two men, although she could gain no significance from it.

Somehow, she slept fretfully through the night without incident, and was relieved when she awakened next morning to find the sun shining through the window. She arose with alacrity, filled with anticipation, for Richard would be arriving at ten, and eagerness filled her with pleasure at the thought of seeing him again.

Long before Richard was due, she

was at the window of the library waiting for him to appear. Her mind raced with excitement while her thoughts ran deep and introspectively. When the door opened noisily at her back she swung round, startled, to see George peering into the room.

'I was wondering where you were. You're waiting to see Richard Redmond, are you not?'

'I am expecting him to come at ten,' Clarissa replied. 'And how is John this morning?'

'There's not much change, I'm afraid. He regained consciousness during the night but seems to have lost his memory. I'm waiting for the doctor to come. His recovery will be a long job, I fear.'

Clarissa heard the sound of a carriage approaching and peered through the window. 'A carriage is arriving now,' she said. 'It may be the doctor.'

Osborne was in the act of opening the door when they reached the hall, and Clarissa's pulses raced when Richard appeared in the doorway. The butler smilingly indicated her presence, took Richard's hat and cloak, and Richard came to her.

'Good morning, Clarissa,' he greeted, taking her hand and bowing over it. 'I trust you are feeling better now.'

'Good morning, Richard,' she replied lightly. 'I do feel much easier, thank you.'

'May I have the pleasure of your company today?' he continued. 'I am at your service, whatever your wishes.'

'I should like to see something of the countryside,' she suggested.

'I should be happy to take you driving. It will take most of the day to show you just some of the sights in this part of the country.'

'I'll warn the servants that you will not be back until evening,' George said. 'Now, if you will excuse me, I think I hear the doctor's carriage arriving. Enjoy yourself, Clarissa.' He departed.

'Come along!' Richard held out his

arm and Clarissa rested her hand upon it. He smiled encouragingly. 'The day awaits us.'

They left the house and descended the steps to the carriage. Richard helped her into the vehicle and then joined her.

'Now,' Richard began, as the coach grated along the drive, 'I don't know how you've felt since I left you yesterday, but I have been unable to go about my business for fear that something untoward might have happened to you. We're going to see Uncle James now, and I shall strenuously object to you returning to Trevarron ever again. Would you agree to that?'

'But how should we discover what happened if I don't return?' Clarissa faltered.

'Have you learned anything significant in the past twenty-four hours?'

Clarissa considered that nerve-racking period. She recounted her chat with Emily, and Richard listened without interruption.

'Uncle James gave me some of the background details to those days and events,' he said. 'He feels that what is happening now has its roots in the past. Have you seen Warner Farand at Trevarron? He's George Farand's brother — a man that is completely unprincipled.'

'Emily mentioned him,' she said, and went on to mention the short conversation she had overheard between George and Edwin. 'I am sure they were talking about me, and I fear that something bad is expected to happen.'

'We must work out a method of ensuring that you are safe,' he said. 'The night is worse. I didn't get much sleep last night because I was so worried about you. So we must employ a more practical scheme. Which room is yours at Trevarron?'

Clarissa explained and he nodded.

'Ah! That's the first window around the left-hand corner looking at the house from the front. Good! Now this is what you must do, Clarissa. When you retire each night, lock yourself in the bedroom and do not open the door for any reason before morning. From tonight I shall be in a position to observe your window at ten o'clock, when you are to signal with a lighted candle to inform me that you are safely locked in. Would you do that?'

'Yes!' She nodded eagerly. 'And I shall feel easier in the knowledge that you'll be close by, awaiting my signal.'

He nodded grimly. 'Move the candle up and down three times on the hour. Now let us try to forget this business and try to enjoy ourselves for the remainder of the day.'

Clarissa was quite content to blot out the shadows that lay across her mind, and they chatted in lighter vein until the coach arrived at Belverdene. Sir James was awaiting their arrival, and questioned Clarissa in much the same way that Richard had done, but his expression was filled with doubt as he pondered.

'I must say that I dislike this situation,' he mused. 'If Warner Farand is involved then you must be very careful, Clarissa, for I fear the worst could happen! Perhaps Richard is right in saying that you should not be subjected to more danger.'

'I don't think there is much danger at the moment,' said Clarissa thoughtfully, fighting down her fears of the past twenty-four hours. 'The situation when I first arrived at Trevarron has changed a great deal. No one knew I was here except my lawyer in London; but now the Farands know the police are investigating and that Richard is seeing me regularly, the risks would be so much greater for them. I don't think they'll risk everything now. It's obvious that I should be missed if I disappeared. An accident would not be easy to explain after what happened in the cove.'

Richard shook his head. 'I don't think you should take any risks,' he said.

'I'd like to try and get to the bottom of what happened,' Clarissa insisted. 'I can't overlook that John saved my life in the cave and is lying badly injured. I'm afraid I cannot turn my back on that fact, and I think I could spend a few more days at Trevarron without much risk.'

'It's easy for us to say there is no danger,' Sir James replied. 'But we cannot judge exactly what is in the minds of the people involved, and even with the safeguards you have arranged, Clarissa will be at their mercy all the time she is in their company.'

Richard stirred, shaking his head. 'Let us change the subject,' he suggested. 'Today I plan to take you sight-seeing in Rynmouth.'

'Quite so, my boy!' Sir James held Clarissa's hands for a moment.

Richard was as good as his word. They drove into Rynmouth. Clarissa was entranced by the quaint Cornish town. Narrow cobbled streets led down to a small stone harbour where fishing craft were moored along the quay. Fishermen were on the quay, many of them busy mending fishing nets and lobster pots. Seagulls called incessantly as they wheeled and dived in search of food.

There was a dingy little shop near the breakwater which sold all manner of curios, and Richard led Clarissa inside to look at the wares on display — sharks' teeth, sandalwood boxes, all manner of marine creatures that had been washed up on some exotic beach, coral and polished amber. Clarissa liked an amber necklace, and Richard bought it despite her protests.

'You must wear it as a talisman against evil,' he said, his eyes gleaming.

'If you place it around my neck I shall never remove it,' she responded, and he complied, his gentle fingers touching the soft curve of her neck and evoking tremors of delight within her.

Richard squeezed her arm, and they were silent as they walked back to the coach. Clarissa felt quite emotional.

She could hardly believe that she was actually out walking with a handsome young man who was little more than a stranger, although she felt as if she had known him for a lifetime. A pang struck through her when she thought of Trevarron and realised that very soon this idyllic outing would end.

'You're quiet now,' Richard observed at length. 'Are you sorry the day's outing is coming to an end?'

'Very much so. This has been one of the best days of my life.'

'We can go out again tomorrow, if you wish.'

'I would love to,' she replied happily.

They returned to Richard's farm and enjoyed a late lunch, and then time seemed to accelerate. Richard showed her around the farm, and before Clarissa was hardly aware of the fact, the coach was summoned and they drove back to Trevarron.

'Don't forget that I'll be watching your window at ten tonight,' Richard reminded her. 'I shall call for you tomorrow morning at ten o'clock.'

'Thank you. I shall look forward to that, and I'll never forget today. It was wonderful.' She looked into his eyes. 'I can't wait for tomorrow.'

He escorted her into the hall, where George appeared immediately. 'Did you enjoy your day?' he asked.

'Yes I did, thank you.'

'And I shall call for you tomorrow,' said Richard meaningfully. He took hold of Clarissa's hand and bent over it in a formal little bow. His lips caressed her hand.

Clarissa's cheeks burned and she found it difficult to remain expressionless with George watching intently. She fancied there was disapproval in his eyes.

'Thank you, Richard,' she said, and her happiness faded as he turned and departed.

'John would gladly have accompanied you if this business had not occurred,' George said, shaking his head sadly. 'The doctor called this morning; John has apparently lost his memory, and I would deem it a great favour if you would try an experiment with me. I'm wondering if the sight of you would perhaps jerk John back to normal.'

'I'd do anything to help John. I shall never forget that he saved my life in the shaft.'

'So he did!' Satisfaction edged George's tone. 'I am relieved that he did. At least it proves that no one in my family wishes you harm.'

'That's a strange thing to say.' Clarissa's heart thudded.

'You may think so. But I expect there is already gossip that a Farand tried to kill you to wipe out the Farand debt.'

Clarissa shook her head, unable to believe that her worst fear was out in the open.

'Didn't that thought cross your mind?' he demanded.

'All I know is that John saved my life. If there had been a plot to get rid of me he would not have pushed me clear of the falling basket.'

'I'm still not satisfied about a number of points that have arisen,' said George grimly, 'and my estate workers are now maintaining a close watch night and day upon the house and yourself.'

'Shall we go in and see John? I do hope his memory returns quickly. Everyone wants to know what happened, and he's the only one who can tell . . .'

6

John was lying motionless in his bed, and there was no animation in his eyes as he looked up at Clarissa. She shook her head frowningly as George said:

'Can you remember seeing Clarissa before?'

'I don't remember.' John shook his head slowly, and there was no recognition in his eyes as he looked at Clarissa.

Clarissa looked critically at the dull bruises on John's forehead, and re-affirmed her belief that the attack made upon him must have been genuine.

'Don't worry about it, John,' George said.

They departed, leaving John gazing at the ceiling. George paused and looked at Clarissa.

'Someone almost killed my son, and I wonder at the motive for the attack. If it was revenge against me, then why attack my son? And if someone is after you then why was John saved after such a savage beating? Was it a member of my family who wanted you out of the way but stopped short of sacrificing John?'

'Surely you can't think that about any of your family!'

'I'll consider anything, and I will find out what happened! But in the meantime we have to be careful. You must try to be vigilant, my dear.'

'I certainly shall,' Clarissa said softly.

'I must confess that I look upon you almost as a daughter,' George went on.

'You could have been my father!' she countered, and saw his expression change swiftly. She regretted her words immediately, but he seized upon them with a strange eagerness.

'You are referring to the past,' he said. 'How do you know about that? You were little more than a baby when your mother took you away to London.'

'My father told me a great deal about

his early life and my mother's.' She had no compunction about lying. 'Why? Shouldn't I have been told?'

'There's no reason why not, I suppose.'

'And if you don't wish me to form a mistaken opinion of the past then why don't you explain everything to me?' she tempted. 'I only accepted your offer to come here because I thought you were a good friend of my parents.'

George shook his head. 'There's really nothing to tell if your father explained everything. I doubt if I could add anything you don't already know.'

Clarissa accepted his words but did not believe him. There had to be something in the past that related to what was happening now. Her father had not mentioned anything about his youth, and she wondered how she could elicit the truth from George Farand. More than that, would she have time in which to make the investigation Sir James desired?

George left Clarissa at the door of

her sitting room, and her thoughts were in some confusion as she entered. Deep in thought, she paced the room, until her bedroom door was suddenly thrust open and a figure sprang out at her. She halted shocked.

'Mrs Farand,' she said tensely. 'You startled me! What are you doing hiding in my bedroom?'

'I've been waiting for you,' the older woman replied, her dark eyes filled with a secretive glitter. She stood before Clarissa, a twisted smile on her thin lips. 'You shouldn't have come to Trevarron! I warned you when you arrived! You're not wanted here!'

'Why don't you like me?'

'You are too much like your mother,' Lydia retorted harshly.

Clarissa sighed in frustration, for here was the past cropping up again.

'You knew my mother well, didn't you?' she countered. 'Were you jealous of her? What happened here in those early days?'

'I had cause to hate her!' Lydia spoke

with such vehemence that Clarissa started back in shock. 'But that is in the past. We cannot bring back yesterday. But this fresh trouble! It is because of the curse that was laid at this door many years ago!'

Despite her fear, Clarissa felt a glimmer of interest evolve at the back of her mind. If she could persuade Lydia to talk then she might learn enough to get at the truth. But at that moment there was an insistent knocking at the door and she turned reluctantly to open it to a worried-looking George.

'Have you seen Mrs Farand, Clarissa? Emily has lost her.'

'She's in here.' Impatience nibbled at Clarissa's mind as she moved aside to reveal Lydia, who came forward and passed her without so much as a sideways glance.

George put an arm around Lydia's stooped shoulders, and despite the smile of relief on his fleshy face, his keen blue eyes glittered. 'Come along, Lydia dear,' he said in a bluff tone. 'You shouldn't pester our guest.'

Clarissa sighed as George led Lydia away, and leaned against the door while her thoughts turned over what had been said. Her mind was in turmoil. Lydia had said nothing significant — this time.

She spent the rest of the day in her room, leaving it only to go down to the dining-room to dinner, which she shared with George. The conversation was stilted, and although Clarissa was at pains to sound natural, she failed miserably.

'Does your brother ever visit here?' she asked.

'Warner hasn't set foot in this house since the day our father died. Being the younger brother, he disagreed with the laws of inheritance. He was always a quarrelsome man, so I have never attempted to patch up the bad feelings that exist between us.'

'Could he feel so badly about you that he tried to do something to John and me?' Clarissa ventured, steeling herself for an emphatic denial.

'That's exactly what I'm afraid of,' George replied.

Clarissa was shocked by his admission, and in the ensuing silence she hoped he would enlarge upon his reply, but he remained silent. She realised he had gone as far as he was prepared to go with this line of conversation.

'How is Mrs Farand now?' she inquired.

'Fine. As you know, she doesn't come to the table for dinner. I'm sorry she bothered you this afternoon.'

'It was no trouble. I was quite interested in what she had to say.'

'What exactly did she say?'

'Actually, not a lot that made sense.' Clarissa shook her head.

'She hasn't made sense for years.' George's tone was grim.

Clarissa sighed impatiently, for talking to George Farand was like trying to find one's pathway through a maze. She longed for a walk along the cliffs, but dared not leave the house alone, and feared that if she asked for an escort, George might insist that Edwin accompany her. So she sat at her window, her thoughts replaying her happy hours with Richard.

Shadows began to creep into the room and she stirred, but was reluctant to retire at such an early hour. And she must remember Richard's signal at ten!

As twilight turned into night, she had to strain her eyes to see the outline of the nearby cliff. Her thoughts were distant, her mind far from the room she was in until a strange creaking sound disturbed her and she jerked around to look for its source. Her eyes widened in terror as she watched a section of the wood-panelled wall opposite slowly open.

An indistinct figure appeared in the aperture, and if Clarissa's throat had not been parched by fear she would have screamed.

'Don't be alarmed, Clarissa!' The low voice was vibrant with urgency.

'John! For Heaven's sake, you scared

me half to death! How did you get here?'

'There are secret passages all over the house,' he said in a whisper.

'And your memory has returned!'

'I never lost it!' His sibilant tone echoed as he came swiftly to her side. 'Thank Heaven you didn't scream when I appeared! I cannot stay long — I've come to warn you. I'm afraid they will make another attempt on your life!'

'What are you saying?' she gasped. 'What happened in the cove? And why are you pretending to have lost your memory?'

'There's no time to explain. If I'm missed from my room then disaster will be upon us. You must be on your guard at all times. Don't you know about the secret passages in this house?'

'If I had known I would have been terrified!' she responded.

'We'll talk later, but I must return to my room before I am missed. See this carved figure beside the fireplace? It controls the secret panel. When I've departed you can lock it against unwanted visitors by twisting the figure to the right. Remember that! Twist it to the right. When I come again I'll tap on the panel. I'll tap twice, then once, and then twice again.' He turned to re-enter the secret passage but Clarissa clutched at his arm.

'John, please wait! Was I the one who was supposed to die in the cove or were they after you?'

'Both of us!' he retorted grimly.

'But you were taken up the shaft!' Despair sounded in Clarissa's voice, and wisps of hysteria surged up in her mind.

'I surprised them in the cave. They had come down the shaft to check if we had been killed by the falling basket. They struck me down, but their blows did not render me completely unconscious. I heard them talking. They were going to leave me in the shed at the top of the shaft until nightfall, when they planned to throw me off the cliff into the sea. But I was discovered before they could return.'

'Who are they?' she demanded, mindful of the reason for her continued presence at Trevarron.

'I don't know — they were masked, and I didn't recognise their voices. Now I really must go, Clarissa. Edwin is keeping a close watch on me, and so is my father. But I'll return, and don't forget to lock the panel when I leave.'

The panel creaked and Clarissa twisted the figure he had shown her. Considering John's words, she fancied that he had lied when he said he did not know the identity of their assailants. John had said it was intended that he should die with her, and she could not understand that. The motive for her demise was obvious — the debt that George Farand owed her. What she could not understand was why the other Farands would kill John, and why. She wished she could contact Richard with the information.

She lighted a lamp to check the time,

and was relieved when she saw there were only fifteen minutes to wait before she had to signal Richard. She checked the door of the sitting room, and wondered if the fact that her suite was isolated in this wing was significant. There was a key in the lock and she turned it, and then jammed the back of a chair under the handle. When she went into her bedroom she bolted the door and went to recheck the curved figure that controlled the secret panel.

She stood at the window, moving the lamp as Richard had suggested, peering out into the darkness. A terrible awareness struck her — she was completely vulnerable. She had enemies inside this great house, and her only friend was locked outside. She felt despondent as she finished signalling, and closed the curtains, her only link with Richard severed.

Sleep came slowly, until later, an insistent rapping sound disturbed her. Pushing herself up on her elbows, she hurriedly lighted the lamp, her fingers trembling. Her breath caught in her throat when she realised that someone was in the secret passage, knocking on the panel.

Grasping the carved figure, she had almost twisted it into the unlocked position when she realised that the knocks were not in the series John had told her to expect. They sounded more like someone trying to force open the panel! She froze, gripping the carved figure, holding it in the locked position while the furtive sounds filled her with terror.

How long she stood gripping the figure she did not know, but after what seemed an eternity the sounds ceased and a heavy silence followed, seeming more ominous than the noise that had alerted her. She slowly surfaced from the depths of fear and released her grip on the carved figure, thanking the Fates that had let John visit her earlier.

She returned to her bed and slid under the covers, half-frozen in fear and not daring to close her eyes. The lamp gave off a dim yellow light that barely held darkness at bay, and she lay stiff and on edge during the rest of the night. Dawn came; birds began to sing their morning chorus. She climbed wearily from the bed, opened the curtain, and admitted bright sunlight that peered into the room and helped dispel her fears.

She was reluctant to go down to breakfast, such was the state of her nerves, but she made the effort and found George already seated at the long table. He greeted her tersely, and Clarissa wondered if he had been in the secret passage during the night.

After breakfast, she returned to her room to prepare for Richard's arrival, and a measure of relief crept into her mind. But when she entered her bedroom panic seized her, for she saw that the figure which operated the secret panel had been turned to the left. Someone had entered the room while she had been at breakfast and unlocked the panel!

She crossed to the figure and twisted it to the right, locking the panel once more, and was filled with a keen impatience to meet Richard and escape from her fears. Time seemed to have lost its forward movement.

On her way down the staircase she encountered John, and paused to look into his face. His expression was blank, and when she greeted him he answered mechanically, while continuing on his way, acting out the part he had set himself to play. Clarissa was dismayed, for it seemed that neither she nor John would be able to get to the bottom of the mystery. She was obviously wasting her time here, and remaining in danger without hope of learning anything worthwhile.

She waited in the hall for Richard, and when a carriage sounded she could contain her patience no longer. Opening the front door, she ran out to the terrace, and was excited by the sight of Richard descending from his vehicle. He smiled and waved when he saw her.

She ran down the steps to stand breathlessly before him.

'Please, Richard,' she begged, cutting short his greeting. 'Let's get away from here as quickly as possible. I have so much to tell you.'

'What has happened?' he demanded. 'You're looking so frightened!'

'I was terrified during the night! Oh, Richard, I don't think I can go back into the house ever again! I spent a dreadful night, expecting every moment to be my last!'

'Calm yourself, my dear.' He spoke soothingly, but his expression was grim, his jaw set. 'Come and sit in the coach and tell me all about it.'

She was relieved when they were in the coach. Richard ordered the coachman to drive on and held Clarissa's hands as she spoke in a wavering tone, recounting her experiences since she had seen him last. When she lapsed into silence his face was showing anger.

'This has gone too far,' he said. 'I don't care what Uncle James says or what you think, there's no way I'll let you return to Trevarron. It's far too dangerous. And what kind of a game is John Farand playing? Who is he trying to fool? Were they members of his own family who tried to kill you both? And how does he plan to gather evidence against them? Is he waiting for another murder attempt to be made in the forlorn hope that he can catch the culprits red-handed?' He shook his head vigorously. 'No! You've spent a terrible night here, and with no worthwhile result. We shall tell Uncle James this morning that there must be a less dangerous way of handling this frightening business.'

They reached Belverdene to find Sir James waiting, and Clarissa repeated a narration of her experiences. When she ended she sat with her head lowered. Tiredness dragged at her eyelids, and she barely heard the ensuing discussion. Richard voiced his opinion forcefully against her return to Trevarron, and she realised in that instant that she could not run away. She straightened wearily in her seat.

'I will go back!' she said. 'I could get the evidence we require any time now, and we cannot overlook the fact that John is still in the house and on his guard. He warned me last evening about the secret panel. And thank Heaven he did!'

'We shall let you to decide what to do,' said Sir James. 'I can tell by your face, Clarissa, you are overwrought, and you really need a break from this nightmare. Take her out for a drive, Richard. Between now and this evening, Clarissa should try to forget about the whole ghastly business.'

Clarissa nodded. Richard sighed as they took their leave. When they entered the coach, Clarissa laid her head back against the upholstery and closed her eyes, fighting against her fears. She stifled a yawn, sank a little deeper in her seat, and closed her eyes. Richard put an arm around her shoulders, pulled her close and eased her head against his broad shoulder. With the comfort of Richard's arms around her and the reassuring sound of his heart beating, it was all Clarissa needed to make her feel secure. She snuggled up to him and let all her fears drain away . . .

7

Clarissa slept on Richard's shoulder for two hours, and when she awoke and found herself in his embrace she was thankful for his presence.

'I do apologise for sleeping in your company,' she said quietly. 'It is the height of bad manners.'

He shook his head. 'I can understand what last night must have been like for you,' he countered. 'And if you are going back to Trevarron later then I suspect you won't get much sleep tonight, so you must rest now as much as you can.' He tightened his embrace. 'I'm quite comfortable like this, so don't give me a second thought.'

The day proved to be one to remember, and as the sunny hours passed, Clarissa became calmer and the terrors that had assailed her began to recede. Richard took her on a long drive that was intended to divert her mind, and she resisted the tiredness that drugged her, looking with interest at every landmark and beauty spot they visited.

Inevitably, a sense of intimacy began to envelop Clarissa, and later, when they entered the coach after looking at a beauty spot high on the cliffs, she was thrown against Richard when the coach started forward suddenly, and he slid his arms around her shoulders to prevent falling off the seat. She blushed and tried to straighten, but he held her gently and leaned forward until their faces were only inches apart. Then he kissed her, and laughed lightly because she was greatly confused.

'I have wanted to do that ever since we met,' he said huskily, his dark eyes gleaming with satisfaction. 'I've never seen a more beautiful girl, even with the worry showing in your face. But you are looking more rested now. I'm not happy with the particular way you came into my life, but the fact that you are here is little short of a miracle.'

Clarissa did not know how to reply, but her feelings were such that she leaned against him and they continued to hold hands.

'We are stopping at the Jolly Smugglers Inn for lunch,' Richard said, 'and later we shall decide what's to be done about our problems.' He smiled at her, and added, 'I did say *our* problems!'

'I'm certain you don't have any problems in your well-ordered life, and I suspect that I have become an intolerable burden on you. I pray you do not feel responsible for me because you saved my life.'

'But I want to feel responsible,' he replied with a smile, and her eyes filled with emotion. 'You must know that I have more than a passing concern for you, Clarissa. Also, I am much enchanted by your sweetness and greatly intrigued by this trouble which now attends you. Life was quite dull before your advent, I assure you, and now I have something worthwhile to occupy my time and energy. I only hope that when we have solved our mystery, you will not go hurrying back to London.'

'I swear I won't!' She drew a deep breath and looked into his intent face. There was kindness in his eyes and an intimate note in his tone. 'There is nothing back in London for me. I never had any friends, and now my father is dead I am alone in the world. I accepted George Farand's offer to visit because I need some time in which to consider my future. Now, with all this trouble happening, I don't know which way to turn.'

'Don't worry. You can come and stay with Julia and me when this business is settled. Then you can begin to enjoy life. I'm sure you will like my sister and, knowing her as I do, I'm certain you and she will become very good friends — and that will make two friends you'll have here in Cornwall.'

At that moment the coach pulled into the yard of The Jolly Smugglers.

Richard glanced through the window. 'I hope you are hungry, Clarissa.'

'I'm ravenous,' she replied with a laugh. 'At Trevarron I can hardly eat.'

'Then you must eat your fill before you return there.' His eyes were watchful as he spoke, and he caught the dart of fear that appeared in her eyes. 'I don't wish to raise the subject of your return to that house just yet,' he added quickly. 'There's time enough to talk it over later. But I cannot help thinking that we are handling this the wrong way. However . . . ' He broke off, shaking his head, and then, upon an impulse, bent his head and raised Clarissa's hand to his lips. 'It is the nights that are so worrying,' he said softly, his breath warm upon her fingers. 'I can protect you each day, but once you pass under the Farand roof I am quite helpless.'

She frowned, and Richard shook her gently. 'Now don't start thinking about Trevarron,' he chided softly. 'I'm sure that by the time we turn back in that direction you will have decided not to return there. Then I shall take you to my home and you'll be safe.'

They entered the inn for lunch, and Clarissa felt almost her normal self when they returned to the coach and began the return trip. Richard worked hard to amuse her, and the coach rang with their laughter, but there was an undercurrent of doubt and fear that could not be dispelled. The ever-turning wheels took them nearer and nearer to their destination, and Clarissa's fear returned slowly. When they stopped at a crossroads, Richard glanced out of the window before turning to Clarissa, his face suddenly serious.

'This is the moment of decision,' he said softly. 'Do we go straight on to my home or turn right to Trevarron?'

'I must go back to Trevarron, Richard,' she said firmly. 'It may seem that I do have a choice, but I know in my heart that it is not so. I can't walk out on John. He saved my life and I cannot desert him. Please drive me to Trevarron.'

'Very well,' he said reluctantly. 'And I'll see you as usual at ten in the morning. Be sure to signal tonight to reassure me.'

'I shall feel easier knowing that you are near,' she replied, and they continued to Trevarron.

Before they left the coach at the foot of the terrace steps, Richard took Clarissa into his arms and kissed her tenderly. She responded instinctively, and locked the precious moment away in her heart. Then he took his leave and she watched his departure with sinking spirits.

A chill gripped her as she entered the house and closed the heavy door, and for a brief moment she paused and looked around, wondering how best to occupy her time until Richard called for her on the morrow. She went into the library, and halted abruptly on the threshold, for George was seated at the desk by the window.

'I'm sorry if I have disturbed you,' she said as he looked round at her.

'Please come in.' He arose and approached her, a great bear of a man whose smile did nothing to alleviate her uneasiness. 'Have you just returned from your daily outing?'

'Yes,' she replied, nodding.

'And you will, no doubt, be repeating the pleasure tomorrow?'

'I have made an arrangement.'

'Good girl!' He surprised her with his apparent sincerity. 'I am sad that, having invited you here, I cannot arrange a good time for you. Mind you, I had hoped John would be in a position to take you around, but, unfortunately, that is not possible.'

'And how is John?'

'About the same, I'm afraid. The doctor thinks it will be a long process to bring him back to normal.'

'And there is no way of discovering exactly what happened in the cove?' Clarissa asked.

'Not until John regains his memory.'

Clarissa glanced at the clock on the mantelpiece. She felt stifled by the atmosphere as she turned to depart.

'I think I shall take a walk,' she said. 'I should like some fresh air.'

'I would advise you not to walk alone,' said George. 'If you must go out, then get Emily to accompany you.'

'I really need to be alone.'

George departed and Clarissa followed him into the hall. She left the house to walk to the cliff path, believing that she would be secure if she stayed in the open, and she could not suppress a shudder as she reached the cove where she had been trapped. Perhaps she was being reckless and unwise to walk alone, but she felt the need to give whoever was guilty of the attack an opportunity to reveal himself. If she skulked in her room all the time, her enemies would merely wait for her to emerge. At the moment she was merely wasting time.

Tension dropped from her as she stood on the cliff and breathed deeply of the sweet air while her appreciative gaze absorbed the natural beauty of her surroundings. The cliff path was deserted, and her eyes seemed to darken as she gazed along the length of the beach and recalled her moments of terror down there with the merciless waves closing in around her. A strange fascination gripped her so that she was compelled against her will to move close to the edge of the cliff and peer intently into the cove.

She saw the mouth of the cave where she had waited while John entered to try and find a way out for them. Clarissa gazed at it and shivered, for in that cave was the shaft where the basket had crashed. A movement in the cave mouth caught her eye and she frowned. Then a figure emerged from the cave and a gasp escaped her when she recognised John!

Her thoughts raced. What was he doing down there?

She shuddered, frightened once more, and resolutely vowed that no sense of duty could drag her back into that cave, although she realised that if John was down here looking for evidence then they ought to be working together. She tried to imagine who might be responsible for what had happened, but no plausible answer came to mind.

John began looking along the foot of the cliff, head bent, eyes studying the sand, and she moved back from the edge of the cliff in case he looked up and saw her. She glanced at the shed over the shaft, wondering if the broken basket had been replaced and, acting on an impulse, hurried to it.

She hesitated when she reached the door of the shed, her imagination frightening her. John had been found beaten and bound in here, and again she puzzled fruitlessly over the identity of the assailant. In all that had occurred, the only factor she could not comprehend was why John had been so badly beaten. He had been lifted up the shaft to save him from drowning in the cove, and that was understandable, but why had he been battered almost to death?

She grasped the handle of the shed and pulled open the door, her heart thudding. Not knowing what to expect, she was surprised to see just a low circular stone wall coping at the top of the shaft, and some heavy beams above it which were intended to take the weight of the basket. It was gloomy inside the shed for there were no windows.

Whoever had planned to kill her had been in this shed. She could clearly remember the ominous figure that had been silhouetted at the top of the shaft after the basket crashed, and it was as if his evil presence still remained, intangibly menacing. She shuddered and turned to leave, the determination that had brought her this far failing under pressure, but she resisted her weakness and forced herself to remain, moving deliberately to the coping stones to lean over and peer down into the impenetrable darkness of the shaft.

A rope ladder had been fastened to an overhead beam, its length snaking down into the depths, and she assumed that John had used it to get into the cave. She listened intently, and when she imagined that she could hear the sound of waves she was terrified.

What was John looking for down there? And what did he hope to find in way of evidence in the clueless sand? She shook her head in frustration and sighed heavily, almost overwhelmed by the musty atmosphere about her, and she experienced a keen desire to breathe the clean fresh air of the cliff top.

Turning to leave, she froze in sudden fear. A menacing figure was standing just inside the doorway, the bright sunlight at its back obscuring its features.

'What are you doing here?' It was Edwin, his voice sullen and unfriendly. 'Haven't you been warned not to wander alone around the estate?'

'Yes, I have.' Clarissa almost stuttered in shock as she wondered where he had come from. 'You startled me!' She paused but he said nothing. 'I saw John down in the cove,' she hurried on, 'and wondered what he was doing down there. The tide is coming in now and he could get trapped if he isn't aware of the time.'

Edwin came forward slowly, and she cringed as he drew near.

'He's down in the cove?' he said. 'Now what is the young fool up to?' He thrust Clarissa aside and bent over the coping, his heavy body barring her way to the door. 'John!' he called and his voice echoed in the shaft. He waited several tense moments but heard no reply. 'The fool!' he muttered angrily, testing the knots securing the rope ladder to the beam. 'I'd better go down and fetch him. He's still not right in the head and there's no telling what he might do.'

He turned swiftly, the movement

surprising Clarissa, and then grasped her shoulders. She pulled away from him instinctively, but his powerful hands held her motionless while a brooding silence pressed in frighteningly around them.

'Stand still,' he growled, 'or you'll go down the shaft!' He pulled her out of the shed. Clarissa gulped nervously, not knowing what to expect. He shook her roughly. 'Go back to the house and stay there. In future, if you want to go out, take a companion with you.'

Clarissa turned and fled in the direction of the house. Her nerves were overstretched and she trembled convulsively. Entering the house, she ran up to her room, closed the door, and leaned weakly against it. There was a buzzing sound in her ears and an encroaching faintness in her mind. Reaction gripped her, for there had been a few moments in the shed when she sensed that Edwin intended to throw her down the shaft.

She drew a steadying breath, and went to the window, where she could watch a part of the cliff top. Waiting tensely, she looked for the appearance of John and his surly brother, and minutes passed before they appeared in the doorway of the shed. Edwin closed the door and they came towards the house together, walking some distance apart, as if they were not friendly.

Clarissa went to her bed and sank down. Her hands were shaking and she felt sick with fear. Had Edwin really intended to push her down the shaft? Despair assailed her, for it seemed that she would have to die before anyone would get the chance to discover what was going on.

8

By the time Clarissa had changed her dress she felt calm enough to face the Farands, and left her room determined to talk to John. But outside the room, she glanced around nervously, afraid that Edwin was near. The total silence and stillness in the house seemed ominous, and she steeled herself to go on. She knocked on John's door, and a sigh of relief escaped her when it opened a crack and he peered out at her.

'I need to talk to you, John,' she said firmly.

'All right! Go back into your room and wait for me. I'll use the secret passage. If my door is locked on the inside they will think I'm asleep.'

Clarissa returned to her room, and a chill stabbed through her when she saw that the carved figure that operated the secret panel had been moved to the unlocked position. She recoiled in horror, and fear enveloped her as she wondered who was entering her room in her absence to alter the position of the figure. Someone wanted the secret panel unlocked, and she did not need to think too deeply to understand why. She moved the figure and locked the panel.

At that moment there was a series of taps on the panel. She tensed as she counted the pattern of knocks, and when she was satisfied that it was John on the other side she moved the carved figure again. The panel creaked open and John stepped into the room.

'I'm sure they suspect that my loss of memory is simulated,' he said, closing the panel.

'Then it's time decisive action was taken,' Clarissa told him. 'You seem to know what's going on. Why don't you call in the police?'

John shook his head and remained silent. Clarissa became impatient.

'Don't you think I deserve an explanation?' she demanded.

'I do.' He nodded.

'I'm listening,' Clarissa said pointedly.

'But what is happening concerns only me,' he said. 'You were caught up in it because you had the misfortune to be in my company that day. It must be a coincidence if someone is trying to get rid of you.'

Clarissa frowned as her mind strove to understand the mystery. She remained silent, wanting him to continue talking.

'Who do you think will inherit Trevarron when my father dies?' he asked.

'Edwin is the eldest son.'

'That's what we all thought until Mother began screaming about the past in one of her fits. Do you know anything at all about our family history?'

She shook her head.

'My mother was in love with Uncle Warner but was forced by her family to marry my father when your mother went off to London, taking you with her. Edwin is Warner's natural son. Warner has always been jealous of my father because the law has it that the eldest inherits. So George got Trevarron while Warner had to be content with the farm next door. Now the truth of Edwin's parentage has emerged, he will not inherit Trevarron because legally I am the eldest son and the estate will come to me.'

'So because you are blocking Edwin inheriting Trevarron, they are trying to kill you!' Clarissa gasped.

'They've been trying to accomplish that for a long time,' John said quietly.

'Do you have any proof?'

'I'm just biding my time to use what I know to keep them at a distance. It could be a lengthy business, but recently they have been getting closer to me. Of course, your arrival hasn't helped at all. If those two manage to kill you and lay the blame at my door then they will kill two birds with one stone.

So, you see, the best thing that could happen is you should leave here immediately and I will be eased in my problem. Go back to London, Clarissa, and leave me with this business.'

Clarissa thought of her first night at Trevarron; could see in her mind's eye the two dark figures meeting on the terrace. Edwin must have been one of those figures, and the man with the lantern would have been Warner.

'I think you're right,' she said slowly. 'It would be well if I left now.'

'You'll be able to come back one day, when my trouble is over,' John said. 'You were born here and your roots go down deeply. But if you leave you should go without telling anyone. The knowledge could trigger another attack on you.'

'I couldn't leave without telling your father,' she protested.

'Be well advised,' he said. 'I'll explain to my father.'

'How do I get back to London?'

Clarissa was so shocked she was unable to think clearly.

'Leave it to me,' he said confidently. 'I'll take you through the secret passages and no one will see you leave. By the time they discover you've gone you will be well and truly out of their clutches.' He sighed. 'Now I must go, and you'd better lock yourself in this room until I come for you, which will be around dawn tomorrow. I'll have a carriage at your disposal, and I'll come for you through the secret passage.'

He departed, and Clarissa locked the panel. Her mind was whirling. But she was greatly relieved, for her hopeless task of trying to gather evidence was suddenly at an end. But she would not go back to London — she would go straight to Richard . . .

She remained in her room, a prisoner of her fear. Eventually, Emily called her to dinner and, aware that she had to keep up appearances, she went into the dining-room. Fortunately, George was alone, and he greeted her quite cheerfully, but Clarissa, watching him closely, saw a troubled expression on his face. She sat patiently through the meal, her thoughts varied. She wondered where Edwin was and what he was planning. John, too, had some preparations to make for her secret departure.

She left the room as soon as she was able and returned to her bedroom, and a sigh of exasperation escaped her when she saw that the carved figure controlling the lock of the secret panel had been pushed into the open position yet again. She ran across the room and closed it, her heart pounding in fear.

She went to the window and gazed out at the view which had entranced her when she arrived, wondering if she dared to leave now and hurry to Richard. She could easily place herself beyond the scheming and plotting of these dangerous people, but she dared not move from the house in case she was being watched.

She glanced at the clock on the

mantel. The next hours would be vital, for she had to survive the coming night and be ready to leave at dawn. But before then she had to make the signal to Richard.

Darkness was closing in when there was a knock at her door. She hurried to answer, hoping it would be John, but it was Edwin, and a gasp escaped her. She tried to close the door quickly but he laughed and thrust a foot forward to prevent it closing.

'Is John here?' he demanded, looking past her into the sitting room.

'He certainly isn't!'

'Well he isn't in his room!' He stepped forward, filling the doorway with his large frame, and Clarissa retreated before him. 'Has he regained his memory?'

'I don't know!' She spoke sharply, displaying more confidence than she was feeling. 'You have no right to force your way in here or use that tone to me. Your father — !'

'My father!' His harsh voice cut

across hers, silencing her. 'I'm sure something's going on between you and John that I don't know about. But I'll get to the bottom of it, never you fear!' He grasped her arm and shook it none too gently. 'John's voice was heard in this room when he couldn't be found elsewhere in the house. So tell me what is afoot. What is he planning?'

Horror stabbed through Clarissa. 'I don't know what you mean!' she exclaimed. 'And how could you hear John's voice in this room?'

'He's not the only one who knows of the secret passages!'

Clarissa recalled the furtive sounds she had heard behind the secret panel, and how the carved figure that locked the panel had been moved into the unlocked position several times after she locked it. Edwin thrust his leering face close to hers and gazed at her unblinkingly with fever-bright eyes.

'You're coming with me,' he said, grasping her arm and pushing her into the bedroom. He held her easily against her struggling and operated the panel, which creaked open. Cold, musty air assailed her nostrils, and she was terror-stricken when he pushed her into the passage. The panel closed behind them and they stood in unrelieved darkness.

'Let me go' Clarissa cried. She struggled but he was too strong and held her easily.

Edwin seized and lifted her bodily. 'I can carry you,' he said harshly. 'You can scream all you want because no one will hear you.'

Clarissa could not scream. Her mouth was parched by fear, her throat constricted. There was fear in her but it seemed to be encased in ice. A sense of unreality held her. She closed her eyes as she was carried for what seemed an eternity through cold, dark air and, occasionally, spiders' webs brushed her face.

She wished John would appear. Only he could save her now. He knew these passages, and was prepared to fight the evil that existed within his family.

Presently a glimmer of light showed ahead. Edwin let her feet touch the ground. 'Walk quietly with me,' he growled, and when her steps lagged he dragged her along unceremoniously.

They moved steadily towards the light, which grew stronger as they approached, and eventually emerged from the passage to stand on the threshold of an immense cavern. Several lanterns were alight in niches here and there in the rough rock walls, and they filled the central areas with a dull yellow glare but left the distant corners shrouded in frightening shadow.

A man was lounging on a flat rock in the centre of the cavern, and he straightened at the sound of their approach and turned quickly to face them. At first Clarissa thought it was George, but when they drew nearer to him she saw that this was someone who was dark where George was fair. She shivered, guessing that this was George's younger brother, Warner, who was supposed to be Edwin's natural father.

'So you've got her!' Satisfaction sounded in Warner's voice.

'She thinks she's being clever by keeping her mouth shut about John,' Edwin said, tightening his grip on Clarissa and glaring malevolently at her.

'What is it that you want to know about John?' she demanded.

'We suspect that he never lost his memory, and you know it.' Warner Farand was big, powerful and bearded. His dark eyes glinted balefully in the dim light, while his black shadow looked like a shapeless monster preparing to pounce upon Clarissa. 'John's been telling lies about the Farand family, and we must stop him.'

Clarissa regarded him with a steady gaze, certain now that John had spoken the truth about these two. She could see that Edwin looked more like Warner than George. They were probably father and son, and obviously plotting against

John, who apparently was the rightful heir to Trevarron. She drew a deep breath and forced herself to remain calm. If she did not lapse into hysteria then she might be able to catch them off guard. Not that she had much hope of escaping, for even if she managed to elude them she did not know which way to run to safety.

'John has not told me anything,' she said slowly. 'I have no idea what this is all about, and if you'll take me back to the house at once I shall overlook your behaviour, Edwin, for I am sure George would be angry if he learned of it.'

The two men exchanged glances, and Warner uttered a chilling laugh.

'I'm sure he would be upset,' he said. 'But that needn't concern you. And to think that if your mother had married him all those years ago then everything would now be perfect in the family.'

'We don't have time to talk,' Edwin rasped. 'We'd better put her in the storeroom for the time being. I've got to get back to the house to find John.'

'Was it you two I saw in the grounds the night I arrived?' Clarissa asked as Edwin took up a lantern and led her across the cavern to a tunnel.

'What are you talking about?' Warner demanded.

'I saw a man standing on the terrace and another man was crossing the lawn carrying a hooded lantern. When Mrs Farand screamed they parted quickly.'

'There are always a lot of comings and goings around Trevarron after dark,' Edwin said. 'It was probably the Gentlemen going about their business.'

'Smugglers?' Clarissa gasped.

Edwin laughed as he took her into the tunnel and pushed her into a small chamber hewn out of solid rock, which had a heavy wooden door across its entrance. Clarissa begged him to leave the lantern and he set it down before departing. The door was slammed with a resounding crash, and Clarissa heard a heavy bolt clash home on the outside. She drew a shuddering breath and restrained it until her lungs protested, and then exhaled slowly, trying to bolster her faltering nerve. One thought was uppermost in her troubled mind — she had to be ready to take advantage of any opportunity to escape. The worst had already happened, so she had nothing to lose and everything to gain . . .

9

Languishing fearfully in the dark chamber, Clarissa's thoughts were of Richard as she fought to keep her panic under control. A sob escaped her when she thought that she might never see him again. Her heart was heavy, and she shed tears until she was emotionally drained. She regained her composure slowly, and finally rose to begin pacing her cell.

She froze in midstride when an insistent knocking at the door cut through her thoughts, and she feared that her mind was playing tricks. But the sound was repeated, and she clenched her hands, steeling herself for yet another ordeal. The knocking continued steadily.

'Who is there?' she called. 'Is it you, John?'

The knocking ceased instantly, and

the ensuing silence was oppressive, menacing.

'Is anyone out there?' Clarissa persisted. 'Please open the door!'

'I can hear you, Elizabeth Kingsley!' a female voice replied, 'and you know what is going to happen to you, don't you? You have haunted this house too long! You cursed the Farands for the way they treated you. But after all these years you will finally be laid to rest.'

Elizabeth Kingsley! A stab of horror cut through Clarissa's mind. That was her mother's maiden name, and the voice out there, wavering and hysterical, was Lydia Farand's.

'Mrs Farand, you are mistaken!' she shouted. 'Elizabeth Kingsley was my mother, and she's been dead many years. I'm Clarissa, Elizabeth's daughter — your house guest. Please open this door so we can talk.'

A silence ensued. Clarissa sighed impatiently, aware that she had to get the door open. 'Mrs Farand, are you still there? Open the door please. Edwin locked me in and I must get back to the house.'

'You made a mistake by coming here in the first place!' Lydia replied in a shrill tone. 'I warned you the day you arrived but you didn't leave. I knew they wanted you to come here so they could kill you and put an end to their debt! But you had to come, didn't you? You're just like your mother. The very first day she came here I could see trouble brewing.'

'What kind of trouble?' Clarissa frowned, her hands pressed against the rough wood of the door. 'Lydia, why did you marry George when it was Warner you loved?'

'My parents forced me!' Anguish sounded in the muffled voice. 'When Elizabeth went off with your father I was made to marry George because he was the master of Trevarron. Poor Warner had nothing but the farm, and they said he was not good enough for me. But we fooled them!' A harsh laughed sounded, with an edge to it that chilled Clarissa. 'No one knows the truth!'

'I know the truth, Lydia!' Clarissa shouted. 'Edwin is not George's son. His father is Warner!'

The door shook under a sudden attack, and Clarissa put her hands over her ears as the demented woman outside screamed and ranted. Then silence came and, minutes later, Lydia spoke quite calmly. 'Who told you about Edwin's parentage?' she demanded.

'Everyone knows. It's no longer a secret. You divulged the truth during one of your spasms. So open the door and take me back to the house. I'll overlook George's debt to me, if that is what's troubling your family. I'll go back to London today and forget that I ever came to Cornwall.'

'You're going into the cove at high tide!' Lydia screamed in rage. 'You'll never be found, and that will be an end to the trouble you have caused.'

'You can't mean that,' Clarissa said.

'Open the door please.'

Frenzied laughter followed, and Clarissa was terrified as she wondered what chance she had with such a person outside. She felt as if she had fallen into a nightmare from which there was no awakening. She caught her breath and steeled herself against cold fear.

'What happened to you, Lydia?' she demanded. 'What caused your illness?'

'I'm not ill,' raged the screeching voice.

'But you are!' Clarissa insisted, hoping to push the woman far enough to overcome her common sense and force her to act involuntarily. If Lydia was enraged sufficiently she might unbolt the door. 'No one in her right mind would do this to an innocent girl,' she continued, and laughed. 'You are insane, Lydia!'

Screams ensued, and the door shook under a flurry of blows. Then, suddenly, Clarissa heard the sound of the heavy bolt being withdrawn. She stepped backwards as the door was thrust open and Lydia came rushing into the chamber, her small figure throwing a grotesque shadow on the opposite wall. Her face was twisted with hatred as she hurled herself at Clarissa, fingers crooked into talons that came clawing at Clarissa's face.

Clarissa defended herself, and the knowledge that the door was finally open lent her desperate strength. She was taller and heavier that Lydia, and thrust at the smaller woman with both hands, trying to push her off balance.

Moving sideways with her back to the wall, Clarissa managed to get between Lydia and the door, and then mustered her strength and pushed Lydia hard, sending her sprawling to the ground. Clarissa turned instantly, ran from the chamber and slammed the door. She thrust home the bolt and then leant heavily against the door, shocked, gasping for breath. Lydia was screaming dementedly inside the chamber.

Clarissa looked around the cavern, wondering which of the tunnels would lead to safety. She dared not use the tunnel back to the house for that was the way Edwin and Warner would use in their search for John.

She studied the tunnels, praying that she would pick the right one. One was larger than the others and, relying on her intuition, she entered it, carrying one of the lanterns and summoning up what was left of her courage and her nerve.

'Hey!' A man's voice called sharply, sending a string of echoes through the cavern.

Clarissa turned and saw Edwin emerging from the tunnel leading from the house. Panic filled her as she fled along the tunnel she had selected. But almost immediately she saw a light appearing in the darkness ahead and realised with swiftly mounting horror that someone was coming along it towards her. She halted in despair.

Turning, she retraced her steps and ran back to the cavern, and then darted off to the left, making for one of the other tunnels. But Edwin was close behind her now; suddenly at her shoulder and grasping her wrist. She was jerked out of her stride and spun around to face him, and without thinking she swung the lantern into his face. Edwin jerked sideways and the lantern crashed against the side of his head. He uttered a cry at the impact. The lamp was extinguished. Clarissa watched him crumple to the ground.

She ran across the cavern and threw herself behind the cover of some kegs stacked near a rock wall. Moments later a figure carrying a lantern appeared from the tunnel she had left and she recognised Warner. She crouched in her hiding place and watched as Warner crossed to Edwin's side and bent over the motionless figure. Moments later, Edwin stirred and sat up, holding both hands to the side of his head.

Edwin arose and tottered around for a few moments, shaking his head and uttering fearsome oaths. Finally, he turned, snatched up a lantern, and led

Warner into another tunnel, where they vanished from sight.

Clarissa sighed in relief and once more took stock of the situation. She went to the tunnel she fancied would lead her to safety, collecting a lantern from a flat rock on her way, and strode out boldly, the rock floor uneven beneath her pattering feet. She picked up her skirts with one hand, for her heels kept catching in the hem of her gown. The ground was broken in places, the atmosphere dank, and she had to fight rising panic as she resisted the chill sensation trying to overcome the unreality of what was happening.

Time seemed to stand still as she went on resolutely, until she saw a light ahead, coming towards her. A gasp of horror escaped her, for she was aware that she no longer had the strength to flee. She slumped against the rock wall at her side and numbly awaited the inevitable meeting. Her gaze was hypnotised by the bobbing light as it drew nearer. It was being carried by a man, she could see, and he was holding a pistol in one hand. Then she recognised John, and her relief was boundless.

'John,' she cried, running towards him. 'I'm so glad to see you!'

'Clarissa!' He was startled. 'What are you doing down here? I've been looking everywhere for you.'

She explained what had happened, and John looked perplexed as he reached out and relieved her of the lantern.

'I don't understand what is happening,' she ended, glancing nervously at the shadows hemming them in. 'Even your mother is helping Edwin and Warner.'

'My mother?' He shook his head in disbelief, and then laughed harshly. 'So that's the way of it! But all's well now, Clarissa. We must go back to where Mother is locked in. The shock of this might drive her completely insane.'

'I'd rather not face her again,' Clarissa said worriedly.

'Trust me,' he said. 'We must do this my way. Carry your lantern so I may have a free hand with my pistol.'

Clarissa took the lantern and turned to retrace her steps while John followed. They eventually reached the tunnel where Lydia was imprisoned, and John paused.

'I'll keep watch here,' he said. 'Go and let Mother out. 'She won't touch you while I am here. Hurry, Clarissa. It is getting late.'

Clarissa went to the chamber and dragged back the heavy bolt. The door swung open and she peered inside to see Lydia crumpled on the floor, weeping.

'Mother,' John called. 'It's all right now. Come with us.'

Lydia jerked up at the sound of her son's voice. Her face looked incredibly old and worn. But her eyes glittered as she arose.

'You've got her, John!' There was cold sanity now in Lydia's voice. 'But Edwin and Warner are somewhere around. It was they who brought her here.'

'To save her from me!' John laughed, and Clarissa frowned as she took in the import of his words.

'From you?' she queried. 'What do you mean?'

'Precisely that!' He leered at her, his whole expression changing. 'So you thought Edwin and Warner were behind all your problems! Well, it's too bad you gave them the slip because they've been trying to save your life ever since you came to Trevarron. I'm the one who's been trying to kill you!'

10

Clarissa could only gaze at John in disbelief, her mouth dry and her heart thudding painfully. Time stood still as his words sank in to her bemused brain. Then Lydia chuckled evilly.

'There's no time to waste,' she said viciously. 'The tide won't wait. You must finish what you set out to do, John.'

'But I don't understand,' Clarissa said. 'If this isn't a grim joke, then you've been lying to me about Edwin and Warner!' She gulped. 'But you saved my life in the cave! You pulled me clear of the basket. And you were almost beaten to death!'

'I saved you from the basket because I didn't want any marks of violence found on your body,' John replied. 'It was all arranged with Osborne. He dropped the basket down the shaft. It wasn't meant to hit you, just scare you out of your wits, which it did. When I left you outside the cave, Osborne winched me up the shaft on a rope. He bound me, and was supposed to beat me lightly to make it seem that I had been the victim of an attack, but the fool goes into frenzy when he uses violence, and he almost killed me before he could stop himself.'

'But why was there a plot against me?' Clarissa demanded. 'I'm a stranger to you, and you can't hate me!'

'I hate you!' Lydia snapped. 'You are your mother's daughter, and Elizabeth Kingsley ruined my life by not marrying George. Now you've turned up, and the fate of my family is in your hands, just as it was when your mother was here all those years ago.'

'But that is ridiculous!' Clarissa protested. 'I don't pose the slightest threat to your family. George knows he can have all the time in the world to repay the loan. And surely you don't expect to get away with this! After the first attempt failed there will be questions asked if I am found dead in suspicious circumstances.'

'We want everyone to ask questions,' said John impatiently.

'Because we plan to arrange your death so Edwin will take the blame!' Lydia said.

Clarissa shook her head. 'And Edwin is trying to kill you!'

'He wants Trevarron.' John's voice was twisted with emotion. 'He's aware that he cannot get it legally because George knows now that Edwin is not his natural son.'

'John must inherit Trevarron,' Lydia said sharply. 'It is his birth-right.'

'And that is why you must die.' John waggled the pistol he was holding. 'The debt has to be wiped out. George won't do anything about you. He still hopes he can pay off the loan, but he's living with his head in the clouds. Our businesses are ruined! We can never hope to repay, so I'm afraid murder is the only answer to our problems.'

'Killing me won't solve your problems. My will has been made, leaving my estate to a distant cousin, so my death will merely transfer George's debt to her, and she will certainly insist on the debt being repaid. You will only add to your troubles by murdering me.'

'That makes not a whit of difference.' John pointed the pistol at Clarissa, and a chill stabbed through her. 'I have to kill Edwin before he can kill me, and the easiest way to get rid of him is to have him hanged for your murder.'

'So Edwin was trying to protect me from you.' Clarissa felt she had to keep John talking in the hope that Edwin would reappear. 'He and Warner must have realised what you were planning, and when they said they wanted to stop you they were not planning to kill you, as I thought. They were trying to prevent you murdering me!'

'John, stop!' Edwin's voice rang out in the heavy silence.

Clarissa glanced over her shoulder,

and her heart seemed to miss a beat when she saw Edwin emerging from a tunnel. Lydia turned, and uttered a piercing scream when she saw her eldest son.

'Take the girl quickly,' she snapped at John. 'I'll talk to Edwin. Perhaps I can convince him that this is the only way we can survive.'

'I've been looking everywhere for you, John,' Edwin called in a tone which suggested that he was trying to humour his brother. He came forward several paces. 'Let Clarissa go and come back to the house with me.'

John uttered an oath and half-turned to level the pistol at Edwin.

'Edwin, be careful!' Clarissa cried. 'He is armed!'

She thrust up an elbow as John squeezed the trigger and nudged his forearm, pushing the long barrel of the weapon upwards as it exploded. The ball struck the roof of the cavern before whirling into the shadows, and thick, acrid smoke flared around them.

Clarissa saw Edwin dive into cover. John stuck the empty pistol into his belt, drew a second pistol, and forced Clarissa on towards the tunnel they had been approaching.

'Mother, go on ahead with the lanterns,' he said harshly. 'Let's get this done.'

Lydia scurried past. John forced Clarissa to follow. She glanced backwards as they entered the tunnel and saw Edwin getting to his feet once more. He began to follow cautiously, but there was little he could do while John was armed.

Their shadows danced on the rock walls about them like agitated ghosts as they hurried along, and when they reached the second, smaller cavern, John did not even pause. They entered yet another tunnel, which declined steadily, and now there was a dank, sea-smell in the air. Clarissa could guess where the tunnel led to, and was filled with apprehension. She kept glancing over her shoulder, and

John laughed evilly.

'No one can save you now!' he jeered.

'You will not escape justice!' Clarissa retorted. 'Richard and Sir James Redmond are fully aware of my situation here, and the police are making an investigation. Your chances of success vanished when you failed to kill me at the first attempt.'

'It suited my purpose to have everyone aware of how frightened you were,' John replied, smiling grimly. 'Edwin is going to take the blame so the more evidence the better.'

Clarissa could almost taste the sea. The tunnel twisted and wound until they entered yet another cavern, and she was amazed to see that it was stacked high with crates, bales and kegs. There were a dozen lanterns alight at various vantage points.

'Contraband!' she gasped and John smiled sardonically.

'This is on account of the debt that is owed to you!' he said harshly. 'If it

184

wasn't for the loan, the Farand family would not have to dabble in smuggling.'

Lydia continued to lead the way, and then halted and held a lantern aloft, leaning forward to peer ahead.

'What's wrong, Mother?' John demanded.

'Who's there?' Lydia called nervously.

Clarissa caught her breath. Had Edwin managed to get ahead of them? Was help at hand? But Lydia dashed her soaring hopes.

'It's Osborne!' she reported, relief in her voice.

Clarissa suppressed a shudder as the butler appeared at the entrance to the tunnel, remembering how he had severely beaten John.

'I've been looking for you,' Osborne said thickly. 'The police arrived at the house a few minutes ago, wanting to see Miss Clarissa.'

'The police!' John tightened his grip upon Clarissa's wrist until she protested. 'What did they want?'

'It seems that Miss Clarissa and Richard Redmond arranged a signal system between them, and, when he didn't see a signal at ten this evening, he sent for the police, who have surrounded the house. They are searching for you, John. Sergeant Cakebread arrested me, and made it plain that I'd help my case by advising you to surrender yourself.'

'Arrested you? And they've sent you here to talk to me?' John spoke stridently, his voice echoing in the low tunnel.

'We're here, John,' a voice called from the shadows beyond Osborne. 'And you can't escape! I have a dozen men with me. All the tunnels have been sealed off, and I'm here to arrest you. Please release Miss Marston immediately and come quietly. Your father is under arrest and we are looking for Edwin. Put down your pistol and surrender.'

John cursed and thrust the muzzle of his pistol against Clarissa's side. 'If anyone comes near me I'll kill her!' he

186

warned, pushing her forward as a shield. 'Get back into the cavern, Osborne.' He kept advancing, and the butler retreated until he was standing in the cavern. John paused, his pistol raised menacingly to Clarissa's head. 'Come out into the open, all of you, and be quick,' he rapped. 'If you give me any trouble she will die here and now.'

There was movement behind the motionless butler and Sergeant Cakebread appeared, accompanied by Sir James Redmond and two policemen. They stood in a tight group while John looked around suspiciously.

'Don't harm that girl, John,' Sir James advised coolly. 'The charges against you are serious, but you would be a fool to add wilful murder to them.'

'She dies!' John said. 'Make no mistake about that! And nothing will stop me.' He began to push Clarissa towards the left-hand tunnel, edging past the watchful group of men. 'Don't try anything,' he warned. 'I've got nothing to lose. Mother!' His tone changed. 'Give Clarissa a lantern. You had better stay here with the rest of them.'

Clarissa accepted the lantern that Lydia held out, keenly aware of the pistol jammed against her side. She looked appealingly at Sir James as she was led towards the final tunnel, but there was nothing anyone could do while she was John's hostage.

'This tunnel leads into the sea,' John shouted insanely, his face contorted. 'You won't see Clarissa or me alive after this.'

'Don't be a fool,' Sir James called. 'Give up while you still can!'

John was careful to keep Clarissa between him and the advancing police-men. 'The end of this tunnel is under water at high tide,' he shouted.

'Give up, man!' Sergeant Cakebread shouted. 'You have no reason to commit murder. Stop before you go too far and we can talk this out.'

Clarissa glanced desperately over her

shoulder but could no longer see the cavern. John was forcing her along, and the sound of her feet on the rocky floor echoed in her ears. She slipped on wet rock and staggered sideways. John seized her roughly, accidently knocking against the lantern, which slipped from her fingers and bounced on an outcrop of rock before falling to the ground. Amazingly, the lantern remained alight, even though it rolled some feet to the left. John cursed and moved sideways in a desperate grab for the lantern, and in that instant a figure moved out of a niche in the rock wall almost beside Clarissa. It passed her swiftly and lunged at John, who was bent almost double, one hand grasping Clarissa's wrist and the other, holding the pistol, stretched out to snatch up the fallen lantern.

The newcomer was holding a pistol in his right hand, Clarissa saw, and the weapon lifted and then crashed down upon John's hand that was grasping Clarissa. John yelled in pain and his fingers slipped from Clarissa's arm. She screamed, pulling away like a startled deer. Her eyes had widened in shock and her surprise increased when she recognised that the newcomer was Richard.

John's reflexes were surprisingly fast. He twisted sideways, the pistol in his hand swinging up in a tight arc. Clarissa cried out, fearing that Richard would be hurt. But he kicked upward, and John's pistol left his hand and sailed through the air. The next instant Richard's fist connected with John's right temple, sending him sprawling into a nerveless heap.

The tunnel was suddenly crowded with policemen, who seized John and bore him triumphantly away.

Clarissa gasped for breath, swamped by relief. But it was all too much for her overwrought mind. She fell into Richard's strong arms, the strength of his body enveloping her, filling her with a great sense of security. Richard stroked her cheek, his lips pressing gently into her willing kiss.

'Clarissa, darling!' His voice was warm and husky. 'I don't know what I should have done if anything untoward happened to you.' He hesitated. 'You have become very dear to me. Can I dare to think that maybe in my wildest dreams you would think of me as more than a good friend?'

Clarissa gazed shyly into Richard's eyes, her lips parting into an illuminating smile. 'Dearest Richard, surely you must have realised that I've been in love with you ever since we met on that dreadful cliff.' She shivered, recalling the awful past, and was greatly relieved that the nightmare was finally over.

Richard beamed happily in the knowledge that his love was returned by this wonderful, courageous girl; aware that one day soon she would become his wife. Clarissa closed her eyes thankfully, feeling the burden of the recent past slipping from her shoulders like a discarded cloak. Tragedy had come close, but Fate seemed to have other plans for her, and as Richard led her back out of the cave she felt at last that they were moving in the right direction . . .

THE END

We do hope that you have enjoyed reading this large print book.

Did you know that all of our titles are available for purchase?

We publish a wide range of high quality large print books including:
Romances, Mysteries, Classics
General Fiction
Non Fiction and Westerns

Special interest titles available in large print are:
The Little Oxford Dictionary
Music Book, Song Book
Hymn Book, Service Book

Also available from us courtesy of Oxford University Press:
Young Readers' Dictionary
(large print edition)
Young Readers' Thesaurus
(large print edition)

For further information or a free brochure, please contact us at:
Ulverscroft Large Print Books Ltd.,
The Green, Bradgate Road, Anstey,
Leicester, LE7 7FU, England.
Tel: (00 44) **0116 236 4325**
Fax: (00 44) **0116 234 0205**

Other titles in the
Linford Romance Library:

NONE BUT HE

Patricia Robins

When Mandy's boyfriend dies in a motorbike accident, she is left alone with a young child and little money. So when her son's uncle Jon offers her a job as his receptionist — as well as a home with himself and his beautiful but spoilt wife, Gillian — she gratefully accepts. But Mandy soon becomes aware of Jon's unhappiness, as well as her own growing love for him. Perhaps if she accepts the attentions of Mike Sinclair, an attractive Irish bachelor, it will help her to keep her true feelings hidden . . .

SPECIAL MESSAGE TO READERS

THE ULVERSCROFT FOUNDATION
(registered UK charity number 264873)
was established in 1972 to provide funds for research, diagnosis and treatment of eye diseases.
Examples of major projects funded by the Ulverscroft Foundation are:-

- The Children's Eye Unit at Moorfields Eye Hospital, London
- The Ulverscroft Children's Eye Unit at Great Ormond Street Hospital for Sick Children
- Funding research into eye diseases and treatment at the Department of Ophthalmology, University of Leicester
- The Ulverscroft Vision Research Group, Institute of Child Health
- Twin operating theatres at the Western Ophthalmic Hospital, London
- The Chair of Ophthalmology at the Royal Australian College of Ophthalmologists

You can help further the work of the Foundation by making a donation or leaving a legacy.
Every contribution is gratefully received. If you would like to help support the Foundation or require further information, please contact:

THE ULVERSCROFT FOUNDATION
The Green, Bradgate Road, Anstey
Leicester LE7 7FU, England
Tel: (0116) 236 4325

website: www.foundation.ulverscroft.com

1